SKY CAPTAIN

32

"ZOMBIE

John

SUPER SOLDIER

Ode to an Honest Soul

"There is no such thing as destiny, unless you mean the kick in the butt, I got yesterday morning to get off my ass and do something about this damned war!"
—General Eisenhower

Super Soldier

Harry landed lightly for once on the tip of his toes. Too easy. Whoops! He had to stop thinking, stop worrying about Hitler's plans for creating a zombie army.

So many bizarre experiments with his own men, let alone the poor Jews that he tortured without a second thought.

He had to stop thinking about it, or it would make him so sick to his soul, he would not be able to function.

Then he spotted what he had caught a glimpse of from above.

A tall, abominable, metallic shape he hadn't seen from above that had been hidden within the thick cluster of trees stepped forward. Its spiked arms swinging, huge conical helmet glaring at him with eyes he couldn't see, but with death radiating from every pore of its super hardened body.

This was another zombie variation created by the insane Doctor Zombie.

The red lens that shielded the Super Soldier's eyes didn't hide the evil intent of the Nazi soldier that was half flesh and half welded to the mechanics of this huge, abomination of life and metal.

It seemed to be waiting for something from him. He obliged.

"Oh shit!" Harry cursed.

He grabbed a grenade from his belt and hurled it.

The grenade exploded against the giant's chest, causing it to waver a bit, but not to stop. It struck its massive, armored chest with its pointed hand extensions and bellowed in German, "Kill!"

"Damn!" Harry cursed. "Since when did Hitler start hiring King Kong to do his bidding?"

The Super Soldier, armored like a tank, towered over Harry. Its armor was slick and shiny, pitted by numerous shell fragments that had accomplished nothing except to give the suit a nicely aged look. Its massive cone helmet had a red prism viewport that made it look like something out of a cheap B movie science fiction movie, except that this creature was part human and part robot and all piss and vinegar armored with high powered weaponry.

"Die!" Super Soldier arrogantly hollered at Harry, raising a narrow fist to smash Harry as it approached.

"Yeah. You just go on and think that!" Harry joked and then lobbed two fists of grenades at the monster Nazi soldier.

This time the huge machine-like Nazi stumbled.

Harry glanced to his right.

Two more of the bastards were stomping towards him from his flank and more from other directions.

"What did I do, land in a convention of assholes?" He joked in German.

The Super Soldiers bellowed at the top of their voice, "KILL!"

Harry shrugged, and then turned his rocket pack on full power.

He shot into the air and the Super Soldiers collided against each other.

"Harry?"

"Copy, Bear," he told Barry over his helmet mike.

"What was that horrible sound you made just then?"

"Hungry," Harry teased."

"Sounded like two tanks colliding."

"More like half a dozen," Harry quipped. "Nothing that two scrambled eggs, half a dozen sausages and a sweet roll couldn't cure."

"Yeah, that makes the both of us," Bear grunted back, his deep voice thick with irony and humor. "So now, what made that sound?"

"Super Soldiers."

"Damn, Cap, you have all the luck."

Long pause. "What are Super Soldiers?"

Harry laughed. "A lot of muscle glued onto Nazi brains that have been hammered to perfection."

"Sounds like a coffee commercial."

"Yeah, except in this case instead of being full of beans, they're full of..."

Al jumped in. "Harry, General Eisenhower listening in."

"Uh...instead of beans, pork."

Eisenhower chuckled into the helmet. "Harry, the analogy doesn't work as well as what you were thinking."

"Sorry, General. Welcome to Base."

"Yeah. About that..."

"Sir?"

"Did you reach the operative?"

"Had a giant German pickle get in the way as you know, sir."

"Yeah. Well, sounds great for a sandwich, but what about our friend?"

Harry swung in a fast arc in the direction he had just fled.

The Super Soldiers were closing in on the person he had come to rescue.

They didn't have a chance.

"Looks bad."

"Bad is unacceptable."

"Don't I know I," Harry replied, already diving back to take on the Super Soldiers.

But the person on the edge of the cliff was not waiting for him to arrive. He then saw it was a woman.

"A woman. You didn't tell me it was a woman," Harry complained.

"Need to know," Eisenhower replied.

"Well, she's in a whole lot of hurt and pain if I don't act fast. Signing off!"

Standing at the edge of a cliff, the woman looked down, then at the stomping soldiers of metal, the Super Soldiers rushing her, and then decided.

She turned and dove from the cliff's edge.

"Oh crap!" Harry cursed, and then poured on the juice.

She fell so fast that the air ripped the screams from her lungs as she wind-milled towards certain death on the rocks below.

Harry swooped down like a hawk and caught the woman in his arms just feet above the nearest rock that would have pulverized her.

The extra weight threw him off course and they both plummeted towards a jagged up thrust of rocks and boulders.

"Mercy!" She cried into Harry's helmet and shut her eyes, saying a prayer for the two of them.

He kicked the suit into a hard arc left. His root boot struck part of the nearest boulder and shredded its side off.

He let out a groan. "I just bought those damn boots!"

He heard laughter in his ear.

He swiveled a bit to investigate her face. "It's not like I ever get paid that much."

She kissed his helmet.

"What was that for?"

She threw her arms around his neck. "For saving my life."

"Thanks."

"Oh! Monsieur, that is just for saving my life; I have so much more I wish to give you."

He felt his blood boil at those words. "No need."

She gave him a look of utter shock. "Friend?"

Harry grinned into her face. Lost because of his helmet. So, he just said, "Do you date Americans often?"

"Yes," she replied in French. "Especially ones with metallic heads that swoop from the sky like Superman."

Harry swept her away in a lengthening arc, until he saw Paris in the near distance.

"My head is a bit softer than this helmet."

"We shall see."

His blood began to boil even more. He needed to head this off before it got out of control. For both. "How about coffee on the Rue Moran?"

She grinned into his helmet. "I'm buying, but sadly the Rue Moran is no more."

"Then where?"

"How about my place?"

Harry gulped. Trying to figure out the right response.

Harry grinned. "Now I know why we love the French so much."

He put on a burst of speed.

She screamed as they whipped through the air and clung more tightly to him.

For a moment he felt his hormones rise even further, but then the image of the woman he had left behind rose like a damnation in his mind and he sighed unhappily.

Her smile.

Her tender kisses.

Her warm hugs.

A world where the Nazis hadn't won yet. Where Hitler was working on atomic bombs but hadn't launched any yet.

Would he ever be able to return there?"

Honor before pleasure was his motto.

He intended to die by it if necessary. But tonight, would be harder than most nights. The warmth of the woman's body against him reminded him so much of what he missed in his life.

He was a soldier first and foremost, but he still had a heart and emotions.

He sighed.

She couldn't have possibly heard him, but she gave him a bit of a nudge against his helmet with her head, as if commiserating.

What a dame? Harry thought.

Honor before pleasure was his motto, he reminded himself as they angled for a landing by the Seine.

When he landed and set her down. She swayed a moment and he had to catch her to keep her from falling.

She flung her arms around him and held tight, crying.

He didn't know what to do.

What do you do when a woman is in pain and holding onto you?

God forgive him, he needed a hug too.

So, he held her a long, long time and neither said a word as the night lengthened and the moon rose high overhead.

And even though a strange sight on the streets of Paris, not a single Frenchman stopped or remarked. They knew of him.

He was a hero.

And heroes needed to be held too. They, as Frenchmen, knew that better than most.

Finally, she let go.

She wiped at her eyes.

"I'm so sorry to have kept you from returning to battle, Captain Harry."

"Harry, please."

She smiled.

He took his helmet off and grinned.

Her eyes widened. "You are so handsome, monsieur!"

"And you are quite beautiful!" He returned.

She blushed and took his free hand. "About the promised coffee?"

"With sugar and milk?"

"And honey," she added, giving him a suggestive look.

While he didn't make love to a beautiful French Underground Leader that night; he did get the best coffee and cake he had ever had in his lifetime and a ton of kisses from her and all her fellow Underground members, who flooded into her apartment the moment she began to serve him coffee.

That night went swiftly.

Filled with friendly chatter.

Rumors of the dread Super Soldiers.

Her name was Marie and she told everyone of how he had singlehandedly defeated a dozen of the dreaded Nazi monsters.

When the last member left, giving her a wink before exiting, she had shut and locked the door.

He looked into her eyes.

She gave him a look he knew quite well.

Honor before pleasure was his motto.

But how can a young man refuse to honor a young Mademoiselle's wishes without losing honor?

She smiled, knowing she had won this battle.

He smiled too, knowing it didn't matter.

He was lost in time; but he wasn't stupid. He could die tomorrow, and she promised him a moment he might never experience again.

She led him into her bedroom and shut the door.

Ode to an Honest Soul

"Honor is dead if trust is betrayed. Love is hollow if it is so easily abandoned."
—Mahatma Gandhi

Rockets

"Rockets!" Harry cried out and everyone scattered as he blasted past, accelerating faster and faster, blue radiant energies lighting his trail.

A nimbus of blue light surrounded his body momentarily as the force field tightened about him, protecting him from the gee forces he was experiencing and his body suit from breaking apart.

His rocket suit was a work of wonder.

Everyone loved watching it, just like we love Fourth of July fireworks, only the energy powering Harry's suit was more like an atomic bomb on a scale of ten; a thousand times more dangerous.

If it blew up, there would be a mushroom cloud and a crater a mile deep left behind to mark where it had been. As for Harry, no one would be able to tell the difference anyway, he'd be electrons spinning around excited atoms. Gone. Poof. Vanished forever.

Dead.

Techs and ground crew hid behind blast shields, not wanting to get exposed to the radiation, which they already knew from Einstein and Harry personally, was unstable and had some pretty drastic side effects, like projecting Harry back and forth through time, from the time of World War Two at a crucial moment of battle there to many dozens of years later in the future where the Nazis ruled the planet because the Allies had been too late in stopping them.

Scary thought, right?

But it had happened and still happening in other time streams as well.

He shook his helmeted head in anger. Why in the world were they allowed to do this? Didn't God know what was going on? Or was he just giving them enough rope to hang themselves on.

He shook off those thoughts. He didn't understand how God worked. He wanted to, but feared he would have to become a monk or a priest to do that, so instead he just worried over it sometimes and most of time just took care of business.

But in this one-time stream America had sat on its ass while Hitler played "Here Kitty, Kitty" with the Allies and beat the crap out of them. America had withheld its hand in battle while well placed agents of Hitler promoted, in the guise of patriotism, vast protests that America should stay out of any war, creating news articles and discussion groups that promoted peace, but not because they truly believed in it, but to subvert the ordinary citizens from pursuing a course of action that would thwart the evil Nazi ambitions.

Millions of Americans refused to fight, to vote for war or to support it. It was chaos. The nation divided. It got to the point where family members were fighting with each other instead of paying attention to what the masterful Hitler was truly doing...knocking off nations like dominoes in a row...with America soon to come.

Also, no one really believed that Hitler would ever do what he said he would. And if that sounds familiar to anyone reading this account here of what happened. Harry hoped they'd give it a second thought, because it happened and more places than you might think.

But back to the story, because Americans were too busy being absorbed in their own problems; their own fears and doubts...they didn't see the trail or want to see the dark and dirty trail of crumbs Hitler left with every speech of hatred he made. He was laying the foundation for the complete and utter destruction of Democracy around the planet.

Well, as it turns out, all those who protested that the man was just a circus act and nothing more, well, they were all wrong.

And everyone paid for it.

Big time.

Sometimes God hollers at the top of His voice, but no one hears it because they don't want to think...to do something besides just exist.

But other times and places...like in Harry's original time stream...same as yours...all proud Americans who saw the horrors that bastard contemplated and was lashing out upon his own people, well they woke up and did something about it.

He didn't know how that war had gone; had ended; but he knew America would have resisted with every fiber of its being if necessary!

But this time stream...who would have ever thought Americans could be such dumb suckers. Unlike in other time streams, were men used what they called the F-Bomb to describe everything from a banged elbow to the way the world ran, Harry came from a more polite time, when men and women had more respect towards each other and in language.

Harry shook his head in regret. He missed his own world so bad. The milkshakes, frosted root beers, curly fries that were actual potatoes and real fried chicken.

He wanted to say worse about this new world, but that's not the way he was raised, but he thought it to himself: Americans who supported Hitler outright and by default...they were responsible for the mess the world was now in.

It figured, Harry laughed inside himself, that such a God-awful place. If this show was being run by God; He had to have a sense of humor, because Harry had no other way of dealing with it but laugh. And pray that he could make a difference here as he had been lucky enough so far to do elsewhere.

"The Great War is not across continents and across the oceans; it is in the heart of man, where the true catastrophe strikes. The true battle to win. "
—Albert Einstein

Sour Grapes

Harry's so-called plate was full of sour grapes. The girlfriend he would never see again because he had been frozen in time on the real world and didn't wake up until she was long dead, and only her daughter and granddaughter still lived. That was the future Harry world, where Nazis ran rampant and destructive.

A future no one had seen coming.

Or didn't want to.

In the first timeline Harry had been flying his rocket suit, the war had not yet been decided. In that war he was dragged away from his loved ones to protect the secrecy of the project he led...to become Sky Captain.

Harry maybe the Sky Captain?

But it's his rocket suit that makes him Captain of the Sky. He was a test pilot who, along with his friend Barry, had been drafted into a top-secret project. Meant to give the Western Allies an edge on Hitler's all too successful war machine.

But now, after successfully learning how to fly the damn thing, he no longer feared the missions as much as before. He knew he could still die. That is just a deal of the cards every pilot, every soldier goes through. You don't get used to it; you just learn how to live with it.

Mostly!

The rocket suit on his back was a top-secret flying machine developed by Albert Einstein, Thomas Edison, and Nikola Tesla. It is pure genius.

In effect it's a leather jacket with a comparatively powerful engine on its back with controls on the chest of the jacket, which can guide you anyway you want. The helmet is an inverted cone snapped together with half covering his scalp and the bottom half louvered to sit on his shoulders and offered eye slits and a mouthpiece.

Cleverly attached inside the helmet were internal mechanicals and electronics that allow the pilot of the suit to have flying control, as well as eyes on what is above, beyond, or below.

That rocket suit allows him to fly faster than even the Nazi buzz bombs. While most scientists were still arguing over whether man could ever fly past the speed of sound, he had not only broken the sound barrier in that time stream, but in the present one as well.

He had flown, not only faster than sound, but faster than Light as well.

How?

By crisscrossing time, like a ham sliced and laid between two sandwiches...the past and the future were all roads he could travel. Not by intent, of course, but as an unexpected result of the powers that Tesla, Edison and Einstein had tapped.

Even without the suit now he could find himself flung across time and space. Fortunately, he was never flung into a hot star, boiling water, or volcanoes so far.

So far.

And this was the future, and his present, which seemed to become more and more of late the one he would live to the last of his days. And lucky him, this time stream had ratcheted odds in his favor by putting together a suit even more powerful than the last and with a force he had never heard of back when.

Dark matter.

Whatever in the hell that really was.

The one thing Harry did know as he rocketed forth was that he had a bomb strapped to his back pretending to be an advanced form of aircraft propulsion that could take out an entire continent or close to it. And oh yeah. Him too.

Figured!

Ode to an Honest Soul

"Truth is often held before the multitudes like a banner, to prove how great a man is, to stir hearts and to steal moments, but in truth...that which is real and truly real needs no proclamation. It is spoken from the eyes and hearts of every man and woman and child since the dawn of time like the laughter of a baby."

—Buddha

Test Flights

H arry eased up on the power juice and dropped to his feet at a run, which he was usually able to manage with a good bit of waving his arms sometimes if he was going a bit too fast, or if too fast, a headlong onto his belly and a bruising, scraping slide that left him in bandages and ice for a week.

Those times almost made him jealous of the armor the Super Soldiers wore. They might be devoid of true humanity; he didn't know, but they most definitely didn't get scratched and bruised like he did when he fell or skidded several dozen yards on his belly.

Ow! That really hurt too.

He managed to land on his feet just fine this time. The crew broke into applause. Some still laughed. And he had to admit it was funny to watch a man try to land as gracefully as Superman, but only manage a half-damaged basketball race onto the court with arms akimbo.

Still, they were kind to him and fast becoming friends. What was life about, if not friends and a few laughs? If he could bring some laughter into this troubled world, then go for it, God!

He thought he had it handled this time after his landing, but then he got overly confident and a tiny wrench...a damned wrench, mind you...he stepped on it and did a belly flop when the weight of his equipment threw him off balance.

He struck the concrete floor with an explosive gasp.

Good thing he had his helmet on, or they would have seen his face go several shades of red.

Embarrassment.

His lot in life.

He grinned.

Still, better that than being an ice cube abandoned in an old glacier, with no grave to mark his death and no future. He still wasn't sure if there was a heaven or not, but he sure believed in God, even if not the typical Biblical one, because it took a miracle for him to survive this far.

Not once.

But many times.

He heard a familiar set of shoes approaching and rolled over to twist his helmet off to see who.

Al...Albert Einstein...stood there, the ubiquitous pipe in his right hand and grin beneath his walrus mustache, twinkling eyes laughing in amusement...but not at Harry. "Seems we need to lighten up, hummm, Harry?"

Harry grinned back at his mentor.

"Like about twenty pounds at least."

"I think we can do that, can't we Nick."

Al turned to Tesla, who gave Harry a nod. He held up a metallic looking piece in his right hand. "Just got this from the yard. Half the weight of metal."

"What's it made of?" Harry asked, as he got to his knees, put one foot down and hoisted himself to his feet.

No one offered to help him. They didn't want to embarrass him. He was grateful as he managed to step to Al and hold out his hand for the metal.

It was light. Ridiculously so. Maybe that's how the giant Super Soldiers managed too.

"A new product."

"What?"

"Aluminum."

"Heard of it. But isn't it a bit too soft?" He asked, managing to bend and twist it between his fingers.

Al shook his head. "We are time treating it."

"What the hell?"

Al grinned. "I won't go into the technical explanation of it all, Harry, but basically it strengthens the aluminum so that it has the durability of metal, but the lightness of aluminum."

"Sounds good to me."

"It is. When the metal's atomic structure is threatened in any way, then the metal transitions forward or backward in time a bit, allowing self-repair. In many ways it's indestructible."

"What's the catch then?"

Nick took them metal from Harry's hand and blew a whistle at it as he twisted it. The metal disintegrated. He eyed Harry thoughtfully at the shock on his face.

"What's the likelihood of a Nazi blowing a whistle at you?"

Harry eyed him suspiciously. "Yeah. What are the odds?"

Nick looked to Al, who shrugged. He returned his eyes to Harry. "About 500 to one."

Harry let out a sigh of relief.

"Fifty in cold weather," Al added.

"Ten in extreme heat," Nick added further.

"Any other good news?" Harry asked.

Nick grinned. "We should have the new suit ready for your next mission."

"Next mission?" Harry blasted

Ode to an Honest Soul

"Philosophers since the beginning of time have insisted there are no such things as mistakes, but what they should have stated is that there are such things as missing the stake you best friend might stab in your heart."
—Benjamin Franklin

Timelines

In this timeline Einstein and Tesla worked together as a team to build the Sky Captain suit, and his weapons. The base was pretty much the same, though hidden high in the Swiss Alps, overlooking a beautiful lake below. In this time stream most of the world was overrun by Nazis, Warlords and Storm Troopers, and the occasional Super Soldier, genetically enhanced monsters that stood over eight feet tall and could take a lot of punishment before going down.

A real lot!

Like twenty grenades worth of lot! Unless you got lucky.

"Barry!"

Harry had found his friend, collecting money from several Techs.

"So, this is where you've been hiding?"

"Hey Cap!"

"You promised!"

Barry turned his face so Harry couldn't see him blush with embarrassment as the Techs loaded his hands with cash. He had bet that Harry would splash down belly first again.

He had.

He won.

They lost.

Harry could see the grin on Barry's handsome face that wanted to spontaneously combust but was held back by Barry feeling guilty for taking the bet.

Harry shook his head... What would he ever do with that man? Bear...or Barry as his real first name was...was a devil in disguise. But a lovable one. He could think of no one else he'd rather have at his back in a tight situation.

Then he felt the rocket pack on his shoulders. He mock kissed his right fingertip and pressed it around to the rocket pack.

"Thanks, Baby!"

Barry gave him a surprised look, and then Harry hit him hard with, "For getting me home, even if my friend didn't save my butt!"

Barry couldn't help himself. "You mean belly, don't you?"

Everyone burst into laughter.

Harry gave his helmet a kiss. "Well, at least, someone here loves me."

Harry hooked his helmet under his left arm to head for the showers. He wasn't superstitious, but he could swear his suit worked better when he gave it a little love. And right now, this moment, it also gave him a way to give his best friend the finger, but in a funny kind of way.

The roar of laughter behind him cinched it. Barry would never live this down, even if he had won the bet.

Ode to an Honest Soul

"Every batter worth his salt knows that when he steps up to the plate, it's not his bat that strikes or misses the ball, but himself."
—Babe Ruth

Rockets

"Harry, why are you cooling your jets?" Barry's voice blasted through his helmet receiver. "Get your ass in the air before they decide to take your new toy away!"

"How about putting your ass on the line for me?"

"Couldn't pay me to do that?"

"How about a million dollars?"

Barry laughed in his rich baritone. "Sure, that's enough spending money to buy one taco. Get your ass moving before I take you up on that stupid deal!"

Harry turned back to the entrance of the Base, as its doors finished rolling up, then began a short run, goosed his rocket pack engines quarter power at the same time as he leaped into the air, a rocket pack superman stretching his wings.

A new wave of applause and cheers greeted him as he shot from the secret entrance of Base. But not for long. The doors shutting behind him like a knife slicing butter on a hot bun told him he was on his own once more.

Good thing the sounds from inside were killed by the sound absorbent materials inside, or all of Switzerland would have been haunted by the sound of the cheers, and Nazis would have been grinning from ear to ear as they came down like a horde of angry wasps to kill everyone and blast the Base out of existence.

Another neat trick that the dynamic duo...Al and Nick...had created was a camouflage metal that overrode the real metal of the door, causing it to blend into the scenery of the mountainside.

"Think of it as a mirror of sorts," Al explained.

"Yeah, sure, whatever you say, Al," Barry had teased. "Long as it doesn't take a peek up on shorts when it's my butt shooting out that door."

Harry had given Bear a big grin. "Afraid we'll see your Mickey Mouse shorts, big guy?"

Barry raised his hands in surrender. "Thanks, Cap, my secret's finally out and I owe it all to you!"

The Base doors shut completely.

Harry peeked at it through his rear scanner and could only see pines, snow, and rock now.

Quite a nifty invention for two geniuses who put the whole design together during a card game over coffee and doughnuts while he and Barry had talked about old girlfriends, the Yankees, and the Dodgers and who would be the next President if the United States ever formed again.

He wished he had half the genius of either man. They were jazzy people too, all things considered. Geniuses with humor were heartening, in a time when most superior officers were a huge pain in the ass with their constant nagging and commanding.

Not that any had done that with him.

Most were in awe with a man who was older than all of them put together yet could kick anyone of their butts without blinking.

The old saying of age before beauty just didn't make sense with him.

He smirked, and then toggled his suit slightly several times in acknowledgement to those he had just left behind. They would be watching him on their stealth scanners and smirking too. It was kind of a running gag between him and the Techies, and another source of income for Barry, who always bet that Harry would forget and lose, so they would get suckered in on the next bet, which would be something more insane, but which he knew Harry would do, and they didn't.

"Come on, Baby! Let's see what you got!"

He gave the suit half power.

You'd think he would have been slammed free of the straps holding the contraption to his back, but the acceleration was unique. Everything that was on him was held together by a small force field that kept his suit on and his body from frying or burning up from acceleration or breaking apart.

He remembered all the speculation about UFOS he had heard from other Air Force pilots about saucers that could turn on a dime. "Impossible!" He had complained. "That would turn any living being into Jello."

Well, here he was now; doing exactly what he said couldn't be done. For a moment he scanned the skies. Were UFOS watching him?

Then his mind flew away in the sheer joy of the thousands of feet beneath him and the ground below whizzing by.

"Ya-whoo!" He yelped wildly, like a cowboy in the sky.

He angled up. Towards the stars. He never flew during the day unless the weather was almost catastrophically bad because they didn't dear let the Nazis know what they had here in Switzerland, even if the country was supposedly neutral.

Had they done so, even Hitler would have crossed the lines he overlooked at times, but never with full force. In the end he would have crushed Switzerland with a barrage of deadly missiles, even as he had the major capitols of Western Civilization.

Had Hitler known of Sky Captain's Base, it would have been the End Game for them, and for humanity's hope.

The Nazis would have finally achieved their final goal. To stifle all resistance. There would be no more free men in the world.

Ever.

Again.

Ode to an Honest Soul

"You can spend every day of your life complaining; or you can stand up and defend yourself by getting into action and making your life count."
—George Washington

Antigravity Trains

Harry angled his suit with a wave of his outstretched arms. The internal alignment motion gears took over, following his motions, correcting for his body position, and taking the new course direction smoothly. So smoothly, at times he felt like Superman. Gotta be careful. Even that hero got his ass kicked sometimes when he wasn't careful.

I might not be Kryptonite weak, but my body is a softie, he mused with a smile.

Easy to do; but complex in construction, his rocket suit was a technological miracle and a wonder to fly. He should know. He'd help design it further after getting tired of his body being twisted around like a pretzel because of some slight imperfections...as Tesla so easily wrote them off. With embarrassment, Harry would forgive him that. But imperfections they were. They had to go, or one day he would be gone.

Permanently.

He'd tested quite a few variations that had given him more bruises and broken bones enough to know that nothing were perfect without testing it first. And since monkeys weren't smart enough to do it, and there were none anyway, and since nobody had thinking robots to do it...least none of the Allies did, then it was up to flesh and blood to take a pounding over and over until everything worked right.

As he turned his thought again about the situation in the world. Yeah. If Hitler wiped out the Base and the underground resistance, there'd still be a few here and there who fought for freedom, but doomed to failure because of the lack of technical and weapons support. Harry was their sole support now.

In fighting and security new equipment for the outlying posts. He had spent many a long night ferrying much needed ammunition and supplies to their friends around the world. Enough so he could almost fly blind to anywhere in the world without looking at his equipment.

Al quizzed him once about that. "It's a mechanical suit; how can it do anything automatically like that?"

Harry never argued with him.

But he suspected Al was catching on...something else was guiding Harry. He hadn't quite figured out what yet, but it was. But whoever was behind the cream and cherry atop the cake of his adventures, he wasn't complaining. Because if it confused him and his allied friends, it drove Hitler absolutely bug ass crazy!

Crazy mad that one man in a rocket suit could cost him so dearly; but Harry didn't mind. The bastard deserved to get ulcers and have a heart attack for all he cared. The man was responsible for far too many deaths and those crippled by this cruel war.

Harry was not a mean-spirited soul, but he was veteran enough to the violence of the maniac that anyone expecting him to sympathize for the person ought to have their head examined.

He didn't believe in devils and demons, but Hitler sure could have qualified for one if someone were taking applications for the position.

Thanks to spies all over the place in secret resistance movements, the Base got reports of the enemy's movements. Sometimes it cost them dearly. Many had died in service to freedom. His prayer was that he could shortcut that time so that no more would die.

But he was only one man.

In a rocket suit.

But Hitler's scientists were good. Too good. They had bullet trains now that used antigravity, much like his rocket suit, to carry important troop movements, supply trains to wherever they were needed. And the blasted things didn't need tracks, which made it harder for them to be booby-trapped and sabotaged, since there were no rails.

On top of that the anti-gravs were incredibly fast and very well armored.

There was no way to take them out, except for a direct hit; their immense engine and cars slung along at breathtaking speeds several feet above the ground, but on a dime could leap skywards to avoid any obstructions in their path.

Including him!

Only a lucky detonation beneath them, or one from above, which was his job...to pin a tail on the donkey. Only that stopped them.

Harry shot above the clouds. The full moon above was so bright he had to kick in night vision, so he wouldn't be blinded by its brilliance.

He looked down, searching for any nearby anti-gravs. As he did, he remembered the time he and Barry had flown a mission together.

Ode to an Honest Soul

"I'd offer to fight this war with the politicians, but I have too much at stake to get enmeshed in that war, when I can't even win the war with my wife."
—Mark Twain

Sabotage

"Hey! I can do this," Barry whined as Harry finished strapping him into the second Sky Captain suit.

Barry turned to eye Harry. "I can."

"Yeah. Yeah. I know. I know," Harry tried to calm his obviously scared partner and friend. "Shit happens."

"Yeah. It does."

Barry had to go to the bathroom several times even before he started getting strapped in. "God, I feel like a student actor all over again when I stood at the side, watching the stage for my cue, and then having the runs right before my cue. Damnit!"

Finished strapping Barry safely. He and Bear, his nickname for his best friend, they exchanged quick chest bumps and Barry ran for the exit from Base, Harry close behind on foot, but safely away from the blaring energies of the rocket suit as Barry kicked the suit to life.

"See you in ten, Harry!" Barry announced from his helmet, his voice echoing in the massive base launch area.

Techs gathered closer to Harry, almost touching him, eager to watch as Barry launched. Some, Harry had seen, were making bets on Barry burning his ass off.

Course the suit wouldn't do that, but it was just a joke that he might end splashing down hard on his butt.

"Watch your rockets!"

"I am, buzz brain!" Barry shot back.

Harry laughed.

Barry was testing the newer, lighter version of the rocket suit. Harry had tested it yesterday, but today Al and Tes wanted someone heavier to test it, to see if it could handle the workload.

They were hoping to create a rocket train for Harry and even Barry to use to bring supplies to outposts where needed.

Harry hoped this worked, because he was pushing the limits of exhaustion with all the night and day loads, he had been carrying lately.

Al gripped Harry's shoulder and said thoughtfully, "I don't know what it is about you, Harry, but you seem to have more lives than a cat's nine."

Harry had laughed. "Oh, I passed nine long ago."

Al had smirked. "Just remind Barry that he's still working on his first and not to do anything stupid."

"You mean like show off?"

"You got it!"

"He would never do that," Harry laughed, knowing that the man probably would once he got the hang of it.

Harry rushed to the exit where Barry had launched from.

It was night outside.

The entrance cracked enough so Harry could peek out and watch Barry's flight. He was probably being silly. Their own equipment could track Barry much better than his eyes, but he had to know.

He had his own suit on for backup.

If his friend went down, Harry would be hard on his heels to help. And good thing he was, he reached the exit the same time as he saw Barry do something the suit wasn't intended for, smash into a tree.

Barry had pushed it too far and fast.

"Damnit, Barry!" He cursed into his throat mike.

"No problem, Harry. Got it! Couple branches won't get in the way of anything."

Barry goosed the engines even more.

"Tell Al the suit is humming like a baby."

"Babies don't hum, Barry."

"This one does!"

"Oh God, Harry!"

The suit became wrapped in a bright light.

Barry's last words were, "Whoops!"

Barry dropped from the sky like a lead balloon, heading over the cliff's edge the Base sat on and plunging thousands of feet downwards.

Ode to an Honest Soul

"The gears of war destroy men's souls; but the gift of life saves it."
—General Patton

Plunge towards Death

B arry worked the controls over and over with the same result.
His engines were kaput.

"Damn tree had to get in the way!"

He tried again to repower his pack.

Nothing.

"I just knew I should have been a Boy Scout when I had the chance," he chided himself as he plunged faster and faster towards what might be certain death below.

Finished.

He was a dead man for sure.

He waved his arms about as if that might somehow make the suit kick in again. But it didn't; he just kept falling. Faster.

Face down.

He could see the crushing rocks below plunging upwards to greet him with a stone kiss.

"Now I'll never collect that bet I made on myself," he groaned.

Barry worked the controls again.

The engines fired.

He wasn't going to hit the rocks now, but there was a huge plot of snow, dirt, and rocks beside the lakes' edge with his name on it.

"Bear, in case there's trouble..."

"There won't be," he had insisted as Harry and he walked to the launch bay.

"But if there is!"

Bear turned around. "What?"

"Whatever you do, don't press the red button!"

"Why?"

Nikola had come running up. "Hurry, our window of opportunity is almost gone."

He shrugged.

What damn red button?

Then he saw it inside his helmet next to the chin switch and tongue controls.

He pressed it.

"Aw shit!" He cursed as the button took effect.

Ode to an Honest Soul

"I'd as soon romance a skunk as be one."
—Will Rogers

Emergency

Harry dashed back inside.

"Barry's in trouble!" He screamed at the top of his lungs. "Emergency!"

Harry didn't wait for anyone to reply. He began thumbed the Base door control and began running up the ramp, not waiting for it to fully opened.

"I'm coming Barry!" He yelled into his throat mike.

But whatever had happened, Barry was out of it.

A medical crew came running.

Harry heard their shouts. He looked back and announced over the Base intercom. "Tune in to my channel. I'll clue you to his location soon as I spot him!"

He leaped into the air, powering up as he did. He felt the reassuring kick of his suit powering up and flew out the still opening doors, angling to go sideways through at the last minute so he wouldn't break his shoulders on them because they were not still open all the way.

He lit his engines full power with a sweep of his hand, and then goosed them. He felt a slight tug of acceleration and then he shot from the entrance in an ascending arc. He turned on his night vision and spotted Barry's trail almost immediately.

It glowed red hot in his sight.

The Red Button

Barry's suit had failed because of the impact to the tree, which he had shrugged off as "no biggie," but in fact was.

It had weakened his suits power link to the rockets.

After he pressed the red button, his rockets had powered up at full thrust briefly, and he had missed the jagged rocks, but then he had shot towards the hard gravel, snow, and light rocks to the side.

He let out a long scream, thinking this was the end of it all.

Then a brilliant blue light erupted about him.

He struck the snow, but instead of feeling every bone in his body smash to atoms, he saw the snow, yards of ice and then dirt and gravel melt away from him, forming a tunnel about him which he was slowing into.

Finally, he stopped, helmet stuck in a huge ice cavity.

"Great!" He muttered to himself. "I'm not dead, but I might as well be. Upside down, head stuck in ice!"

He heard a sound behind him.

"Help!" He tongued his helmet speaker and yelled, "Help!"

"Barry!"

"Harry, I fell down and I can't get up."

"You jerk! Scared another nine lives off me."

Barry's helmet temp monitors began to drop dramatically. "Hurry, my thermals are dropping."

"On it, bud."

"Better or I'll turn into a fudge Popsicle!"

Harry landed beside the tunnel. His feet pressed down into the deep snow. He trudged forward slowly through it; it felt like wading through thick water. He stopped at the edge of the tunnel and held a flash over it.

The sides lit up, revealing ice, dirt, and rock nicely frozen together, forming a long tunnel but with no sign of Barry. "You found the red button, I see."

"Yeah. But next time tell me what it's for, it almost killed me!"

Harry laughed. "Don't blame that button on your flyboy antics, pal."

"Sorry, being Superman is God-awful crazy nuts!"

"Yeah. Read you on that one, Bear."

"So now what? My brain is starting to swell up from all the blood draining into it."

"Yoga's good for you."

"This isn't yoga, Cap, this is Humpty Dumpty."

"Close enough."

"Easy for you to say!"

Harry chuckled. "Look on the bright side, Barry. You're alive."

"Yeah. Yeah. But you're not upside down and freezing your family jewels off!"

"Don't worry; some doll will take mercy on you."

"Fat chance of that ever happening."

Harry was examining the grounds about them. The medical team should be tracking him. So, they couldn't be too far off. He just had to keep Bear positive. The more he bitched, the more likely he'd be okay and not go doing something stupid.

"And you almost had me believing they were too big to ever get hurt."

"Harry, kiss my big brown ass!"

"Base is listening."

"And they can too!"

Harry grinned.

It was working. Now if only the team would hurry up and arrive.

Ode to an Honest Soul

"You can bandy about fame all day and all night, but the true measure of a man isn't what he's accomplished in the world, but what he's accomplished in the transformation of himself.

"As for me, a nice cigar will do nicely, thank you."

—Groucho Marx

Rescue Operation

Harry moved closer to investigate the tunnel that Barry's powerless plunge had created. "That's steep and deep."

"Just like I love my women!"

"Not a time to do bad jokes."

"Not joking."

"Then just shut up."

"Can't do that. I am about to throw up."

"Don't do that."

"Why?"

"You'll drown."

"Yeah. There's that. But just saying."

"Understand, pal."

"Some pal. If you were a real pal, you would never have let me do this stupid thing in the first place."

"Aren't we forgetting the fact that you volunteered and then locked me in my room so I couldn't get out and stop you?"

"Yeah. There's that too."

"So, deal with it."

"Harry, are fingers supposed to turn blue?"

"On Christmas morning."

"Funny. How about toes?"

"Easter."

"Now you've really got me worried."

"Me too. You shouldn't be able to see them at all."

"I got eyes behind my head."

"What about the rest of you."

"Good imagination."

Harry chuckled. "Ever the joker."

"Only on Sundays."

"It's not Sunday."

"So! What the hell's that got to do with the price of bananas?"

Harry turned on his rockets again and used them to start blowing snow and dirt away from the hole Barry had made. Maybe if he could widen it more, he could make a path down to free Barry.

But it was a mistake. The vibration of the powered suit engines and the flaring of the antigrav forces on the tunnel was loosening more than the snow and dirt. It was causing the mountainside next to it to begin loosening, breaking apart.

He hastily turned off power before Barry got buried even worse than he was. The overlapping snow caught above the hole began to loosen as the side snow loosened. Heavy boulders and a huge slope of snow moved ever so slightly.

"Don't worry. Don't worry," he told himself, forgetting to mike off.

"Worry about what?"

"Barry, if you joke again, I'm going to let this mountain side melt down and bury your sorry ass forever!" Harry warned him, commed off, and then cursed. "Damnit, Harry! Think! Think!"

"Like you were," Bear responded with a touch of regret in the words.

Harry recoiled a moment. As he had been a long time ago. Frozen in ice, just like Bear was in danger of here. He shook off the fear he had momentarily felt with the growing memories, then snapped irritably," "Touché!"

"Shutting up. And sorry, Cap. You didn't deserve that."

"Vent all you want."

"Oh, don't worry about that, I'm just warming up." The sound of teeth chattering came into Harry's helmet. "Freezing I mean."

"Hang on, Barry; I'm shoveling as fast as I can." Harry lied.

"Where are the techies when you need them?"

"A thousand miles away."

"And the Meds?"

"On their way."

"Yeah. Happens a lot to guys like me."

"How so?"

"You know...I'm black."

Harry roared with laughter.

"What's so funny?"

"The only thing black about you is your attitude; the rest of you a nice creamy chocolate."

"Thanks a lot, that's really encouraging.'

"You're welcome, buddy."

Harry slipped carefully into the tunnel. By chimney walking, he was able to slowly descend. Where the ice was thickening, he turned power back on, but lightly.

Step by step he was breaking a path up for Bear and himself to reach him.

"What's that sound, Harry?"

"My heart beating."

"Why?"

"Because I'm trying to reach you, shit head!"

"Oh!"

Harry felt bad. "Sorry."

"I know you are, pal. Me too. I should have listened to you better."

"Likewise."

"Why you say that?"

"You wouldn't have had to lock me in my room then."

Bear broke into laughter.

Harry stopped blowing the tunnel open. He took his helmet off and turned his flash on again. The palm light showed a shape in the freezing snow below. Barry!

Barry's huge feet.

"Never knew you were related to the Abominable Snowman, Bear."

"Yeah. Second cousin. Why?"

"I think I see your feet."

"Hope you can't smell them. Didn't wash them this last week."

"Shame on you."

"Yeah. As if anyone would notice, hardly anyone of us washes up as much as we should with all the damned emergencies, we have all the time!"

"Second that."

Harry began digging at the remaining ice and snow with his gloved hands. "Sooner or later, we'll have better times."

"Yeah. When we blow that bastard Hitler to smithereens maybe."

"Why maybe?"

"Because if he's like Al Capone was, he's got a mob of soldiers behind him all itching to take his place and take over the Big Show."

"You're so heartwarming."

"I try."

Harry shouted in triumph.

"Feel that!"

"Don't feel a thing."

Harry got worried.

He had reached Bear's right boot and gently pulled it free. He hurriedly put it back on.

"Now?"

"What are you doing up there?"

Harry eyed the remaining ice and snow covering Bear.

Where was that med team, Damnit?

He eyed the huge overhang of ice and rock above the hole. If he wasn't careful, it could all break free and tumble into the hole, crushing Barry and him too if he wasn't careful.

But careful wasn't his middle name or his first. He had to save Bear. He was suffering from hypothermia and if he didn't get his friend to Base soon, he might lose his limbs or worse.

Harry felt his ache pound for a moment in pain.

I won't let that happen!

"Barry, almost to you."

"Just make sure you don't cook my tootsies if you're thinking of warming them up with that suit engine of yours. I'm kinda attached to them."

Harry laughed. "Then we could have popcorn."

"Funny. Lame." Bear responded, his voice sounding weaker than before. "But mainly lame."

"Bear you all, right? I can barely hear you."

"I'm having a hard time breathing. And I can't even feel my tongue anymore and I'm using it to talk to you."

"Don't worry; I'll have you out in a jiff!"

"Getting a bit warm in here too, Harry."

"Yeah. It's just balmy as hell out here too." Harry replied. "I got pretty nurses lined up for a mile applying to work at our ice cream stand."

"Don't even go there, you monster."

"What? Hate ice cream?"

"No, hate eating it alone."

"No problem, pal. Almost there."

And he did.

Bear's legs were free now.

He began working on his waist to his shoulders.

Then the tunnel went deep black.

Ode to an Honest Soul

The richest knowledge is not born of a book or found on an antique shelf of a library.

It's found in the heart of man.

The love of friendship.

—Sherlock Holmes

Super Soldier

"**D**amn!" Harry cursed.

"Can't hear you, Harry."

Bear was worried. He never said Harry at times like this unless he was scared or worried. He sounded both!

"I've got a little problem."

"What! Betty Boop not wanta audition for your talent show?" Barry quipped, making gagging sounds between each word. "Sorry, wanna throw up. Wanna breathe. Don' know which to do."

"Do? Do either but hang in there!"

"Does standing on your head qualify me for hanging in there?"

Harry grinned, and then his awareness of what might have caused the blocking of the light above returned. He didn't dare use his flash to look upwards.

Something...perhaps his sixth sense as Al called it...was acting up.

"So, what kind of problem, Harry?" Bear asked, his voice sounding tired this time and even more faint.

"Bathroom."

"Hell, Harry, I'm way beyond that. I froze mine an hour ago."

"Hasn't been an hour."

"Feels like it," Bear wheezed, his voice fainter still.

Harry pushed the gain in his helmet with his tongue, so he didn't lose Bear.

"Funny. No, a bit bigger than that."

Harry reached for his side arm, and then realized it was lying inside the suit jacket, all bright, clean, and shiny.

"Shoot it."

"Another small problem."

"What small problem?"

"I can't reach my weapon."

Bear didn't respond.

"Oh hell!" Harry growled.

He risked the unthinkable, grabbed Bear's boots and powered up.

He had to be careful, or he might pull Bear's legs out of their sockets, or the bones of his feet.

Bear began to pull free.

Harry almost yelled "Victory!"

The shadow over him moved slightly, revealing a touch of light.

He risked a look.

"Shit!" He cursed.

Bear didn't respond.

But above Harry stood a Super Soldier. It was missing an eye, and he could see some of its metallic brain pan gleaming on its left side, where something had gashed the skin away. The Super Soldiers were genetically enhanced soldiers, but also physically as well, a combination of metal, electronic circuits and wildly firing genomes.

Hitler had created them during the first nuclear strikes on America. They were near invulnerable when up against one. It took close combat and well-placed explosives to stop them.

Harry was close to freeing Bear entirely, but if he didn't respond to this new threat, they both might die.

He powered up a bit more and felt Bear breaking free. He gently let go after the snow and rock on the sides filled the hole Bear had been stuck in.

A Super Soldier stood above him, and he didn't have any explosives. If he didn't do this right, the thing would kill him and Bear both.

Damn!

But he didn't' have any explosives. But he also wasn't sure if the creature knew he was in the hole or not. It had looked, but it didn't use any kind of light. Harry would be lost in the shadows of the depths to the creature.

Unless...

And that word bothered the hell out of him.

Unless it had sensors that could detect him.

"Crap!"

"What's your problem look like?" Bear asked, his voice still weak.

Harry spoke a bit more softly into his throat mike. "Big. And it's closing in."

"That's no problem."

"It's big."

"How big?"

"You know those ice cream cones you and I used to get in the cafeteria."

"The ones that were almost as tall as us."

"Well, yeah. But this is bigger. Way bigger."

"What are you talking, Harry?"

"Super Soldier!"

Barry groaned. "Oh, we are so..."

"Don't make any movements, Barry, I'll try to lead it away from you."

"As if I could move!" Bear complained. He knew Harry never used his real first name unless the situation was tight. And considering his upside-down position, it couldn't get any tighter, except it had.

Super Soldier. *How life can suck sometimes!*

"Remind me to repeat that next time you brag about your moves."

"I'm going to kill you when I get outta here, pal."

"Be my guest, but you might have to wait in line. This super soldier looks like he's first."

Harry slowly turned about, so he was facing the entrance to the tunnel Bear was in.

Harry powered up and shot towards the huge bulk blocking his view.

God! He hoped his helmet could take the impact.

Then he remembered the red button. The one he had joked to Bear about so the big guy would remember.

He tongued his red button.

He burst from the tunnel; his body lit up like a blue lit Christmas tree and slammed into the Super Soldier's chest. It had been leaning over to see better.

The Super Soldier fell backwards, landing hard on the bank of the lake, sliding several yards, scooping up loose snow and hard frozen gravel in its wake.

Harry landed on his feet.

The Super Soldier sat up, revealing that one eye was dangling from its socket. It tried to reattach the red lens that usually covered its eyes, but it was broken and fell aside again.

The Super Soldier made a roar like an aggravated lion, and then shoved its loose eye back into its socket. The eye promptly popped free again and dangled once more towards the snowy ground.

Harry used the distraction to snatch up a bunch of snow with rocks in it, packed it tight and flung it into the good eye.

"Roar!" The Super Soldier screamed, temporarily blinded by the substance in its good eye.

Blinded, at least momentarily, Harry had it off guard as he launched into the air again full power and struck the soldier in its midsection, knocking it backwards. It teetered on the edge of an icy chasm that fell hundreds of feet into darkness.

Then it regained its balance and as Harry rushed to knock it into the chasm, it swats him away, like an irritating fly.

Harry flew and struck a huge frozen rock. He lay stunned there, his senses reeling while the Super Soldier struggled to get its other eye back into its socket. It also looked for a weapon. Its weapon belt was empty. Whatever had happened to it, it was weaponless. But for a creature like that, it didn't need much of a weapon, its body was a pretty good stand in. It could crush Harry's skull if it managed to get past his body armor shield with its conical arms and hands.

Harry tried to get up, but the weight of his rocket engines was too much to bear now. The swat, even though it hadn't crushed him...the shield had taken most of the blow...still had knocked the wind out of him.

So, still trying to recover his senses fully, he looked about for some kind of weapon he might use.

His right hand grazed something rough.

He looked.

A broken branch. Frozen solid.

A giant shadow fell across him, blocking the moon's light.

He rolled onto his back and thrust the ice branch upwards as another one came crashing down.

The two branches disintegrating pelting him and the Super Soldier with ice debris.

Harry cried out.

His shield was down.

Some of the branch had struck his right shoulder.

"Crap!"

The super soldier roared angrily as Harry rolled to his right as a huge metallic arm struck downwards, missing him, and breaking some of the boulder behind him into pieces.

The other arm was swinging downwards, and it wouldn't miss.

Harry took a desperate measure and powered up.

The huge arm smashed into the boulder breaking it into a thousand pieces, but Harry was gone.

Spinning off like a firework gone awry.

And worse yet, he was shooting sideways towards a huge pine.

He'd be lucky if he didn't break every bone in his body from the impact.

Ode to an Honest Soul

I'd like to think that when my time comes, I won't go weeping in the night over what I've lost, about what I could have done that I did not.

Instead, I'd prefer to think I would march proudly into the Light knowing that I did my damned best and if you don't like it, that's your problem, I'm with the angels now.

—Nikola Tesla

Battle On

Harry smashed reverse powered his engines at the last possible moment and instead of going splat against the huge tree trunk, he struck a large branch and collapsed flat on his face into the soft snowy ground.

He would have groaned in pain, but he didn't have any air in his lungs.

"Crap!" He finally managed, half sitting up, using his hands to prop him. He saw stars. His back felt like someone was driving a nail through his spine. His right arm felt like it had been torn from its socket; the raw nerves were blasting him with searing pain.

He glanced around quickly, assessing his situation.

The Super Soldier seemed as stunned as him. Maybe the power surge it had used to smash the boulder had short circuited some of its powers. But he wasn't going to hang a prayer on him getting off that easy. He saw a chance to turn things around for himself. He struggled to his feet, his spine groaning in pain, his right arm threatening to cause him to black out.

The super soldier wasn't stunned. Its attention was on the hole.

On Bear below.

No!

"Hey Zombie!" Harry shouted, using his helmet's speaker to blast it out.

The Super Soldier stiffened as if struck by a blast and slowly turned around, knocking its conical hands together, as if preparing to do something nasty to Harry.

And it probably would if it could close on him.

Though Doctor Zombie had lobotomized the poor suckers stuck in these machines, until they were nothing more than zombies following orders, evidently he had left the ability to be insulted within them.

Something only a sadistic bastard like that man would even think of doing.

56

Harry had just called the bastard a zombie. Worst insult a Nazi could get from an American. Even Hitler hated it!

The distraction had worked.

Now, if only the rest of his hasty plan would.

He tongued the power controls, praying the suit wasn't too battered. It lit up, casting a blue glow on the white snow about him.

The Super Soldier charged him.

Harry waited until it was so close, he could smell its armor, then launched straight up and to the left.

The Super Soldier smashed into the pine.

The impact of its tremendous weight was so great that the tree split in half, taking down Harry with it as

he was passing through the branches on foot from the perch he had landed on.

He had been counting on the soldier's weaker mind to think he had kept going. Not to mention its broken eye socket. It had to be in a lot of pain. He wasn't certain how much pain they felt; as they were so much metal and electronics; but some semblance of humanity remained, or his insult wouldn't have made an iota of difference.

The Super Soldier stood frozen against the split tree trunk, as if reconsidering its options.

Harry lay beneath the fallen limbs he had been behind, praying he wouldn't be noticed. But instead of charging blindly, the super soldier just stood there. Silent and foreboding.

Harry remained silent. Think. Think. What was this monster going to do next? Something changed in the equation, Harry realized. This soldier was not just super mean and super strong, but also clever. Which meant it was one of the newer ones with the enhanced brains.

Oh crap! I am so screwed if I'm right!

He felt, rather than heard the movement behind him. He rolled aside as a huge fist punched past his face and smashed into the side of the tree; he was near. The tree shook from the violence of the blow and split down the middle.

Harry rolled a new direction as the giant soldier kicked at his face. He caught the foot and twisted. The giant soldier roared and collapsed to the ground. It got up again, its face glowering with intense hatred, and eagerness. Eagerness to smash him to a pulp.

Harry had to stop it somehow.

He was deathly afraid now that Barry was no longer alive. His friend wouldn't have lost a moment in saying something more if he could.

He shrugged off his fear.

Enough to face now.

Harry backed up but kept his eyes on the Super Soldier. Harry's suit was powered down. The red button wouldn't work twice. It could only be used once.

"You won't need it more than once," Al had reassured him.

He had given Al a questioning look, but Al had just walked away. *He's always right,* Harry had thought at the time. So, he didn't push it.

"Look, big guy, I know we kinda started out a bit on the cold side of things," Harry taunted. "So why don't we just kiss and make up like good little boys? Whatcha say? Huh? Huh?"

The giant metallic warrior rocked forward and then steadied itself.

Even Super Soldiers have battle fatigue, Harry thought.

The super soldier shoved its loose eye back into its socket and he felt as if the man, or creature, whatever it was, was scrutinizing him closely, maybe scanning him in some way to check out his truthfulness. Or maybe he just couldn't understand a word Harry had said.

Harry paused. What was wrong? Why was it just standing there, as if it had forgotten all about him?

Then chest of the Super Soldier burst outwards, a huge fist with a stone attached to it, poking through. The fist plucked out of view.

The super soldier slowly began toppling towards him. Harry threw himself out of the way as the soldier fell to the ground where he had laid.

He heard the medics coming down the slope. They would be here any minute.

Harry stood in horror, his eyes caught in a kind of bizarre fascination as yellow and red blood poured from the wound in its back. Yellow blood?

The giant soldier twisted its helmeted head towards Harry. It's one intact eye glowed with fierce hatred and angers a long moment, then the light went out in it and the Super Soldier stiffened.

Whatever it was truly. It was gone. Its consciousness fled from Harry's world.

Harry looked up at the person responsible for the Super Soldier's death.

Bear dropped the sharp stone in his hand.

"How's that for a bit of fisticuffs, Cap?"

Harry grinned. "I like it when a man cuts to the chase."

Bear grinned. "Especially when it goes to the heart of things."

They both chuckled.

Barry's rocket engines were still glowing. He had powered them full when he smashed the rock into the Super Soldier's back and punched through its heart.

"That was a big risk, Bear."

"What's a little pain between friends?" Bear quipped.

"I can't seem to let go the rock. A little help please?"

Harry got up, groaned, and hobbled over. He gently disengaged Bear's fingers from around what remained of the rock.

"You dumb shit! You coulda hurt yourself."

"Look who's talking!" Bear shot back with a big grin.

They threw arms around each other, t hen both let out cries of pain and quickly let go.

"Old men!" Bear growled.

"Not that old!" Harry reminded him.

They both looked at the fallen Super Soldier.

Bear's face clouded a moment.

"What's wrong?"

Bear looked at Harry. "Harry, I'm probably just hallucinating, but I could swear that when I put the rock through its heart it said something."

"Squeal of pain?"

"No."

Bear was silent. He didn't want to say.

"Bear?"

Bear looked up, a tear in both his eyes. "Momma. It said Momma."

"Think you can fly back?" Harry asked, desperately wanting to change the topic.

Barry shook his head. That power fist move I made fried the circuits. He sniffed. "Still smell like burnt rubber."

"How about I fly, and you ride?"

"Last time we did that, you busted my ass."

"I got it, buddy. Won't happen again." Harry promised.

Barry gave him a look of utter disbelief. "You're sure about that."

"Would I ever lie to you, Barry?"

"Yeah!"

Harry laughed.

Bear sighed unhappily, and then got behind Harry. "I don't like the way this looks. Land me outside the entrance."

"Why?"

Bear wrapped his arms around Harry's neck and snuggled tight. "Just take the shit off, will you?"

Harry warmed up his rockets.

He and Bear began turning awkwardly towards the chasm the Super Soldier had almost fallen in.

"Anytime now, Harry."

"Need some more time."

They were at the chasm's edge.

"Harry!"

Harry's rockets cut in.

They were already over the drop and plunging. Harry gave the suit everything it had. It righted him and Bear and with Bear clinging to him like a long-lost lover, they shot into the sky. Past the fallen super soldier.

Let the medics take care of the body. Maybe they could even learn something from the fallen soldier.

Normally, Hairy would tease the hell out of Bear when they got in a situation like this, but not tonight.

He had weightier things on his mind.

"Momma!"

He chilled to his core.

What or who was Hitler putting into his Super Soldiers?

He shuddered in horror. Was he using children to man the suits?

"Remind me not to fly these damned suits anymore, Harry."

"Sure thing."

Harry darted a glance back at the fallen super soldier as they arced upwards.

He had to wonder if the man had any shred of humanity left in his soul. A family back home. A wife. Children? Or was he a...

He shuddered again, his soul chilling as if the devil had touched it.

A child!

Dear God, please no, he prayed.

He'd never know. But he'd always wonder.

"Hurry, Harry, my toes are freezing!"

"Then why did you take your boots off?"

"I didn't! You did!"

"Oh, right. Sorry 'bout that."

"You owe me."

"For what?"

"Letting me save you."

Harry and Bear broke into laughter.

"Not much longer, pal."

"Sez you, who are all nice and warm."

Harry said nothing about his shredded jacket where the freezing night air that was bleeding through the rip in the side of his flying suit, or the red-hot arcs of pain in his right shoulder that Bear was putting most of his weight on.

He was a soldier.

It was his job.

It was all part of the game.

Fight on.

Joke.

Fight on.

Live just a bit longer.

"My toes!" Barry complained again.

"Think popcorn," Harry joked.

"I hate you!" Bear snapped back.

"Yeah. And I love you too!" Harry shot back as he gave the suit very bit of juice he could spare.

Base came into view, and he angled for it.

What a night!

Ode to an Honest Soul

"To be honest, I don't give a damn about your war. I only care about the ones who are hurt by it and you!"
—Sky Captain

THE ZOMBIE FACTORY

The Wrong Battle

Captain Harry Morgan was Sky Captain. A man dedicated...now...through two World Wars, both of which the Nazis won. Born in a time and place where none of that had happened, yet somehow thrust into alternate futures, where he had to face the cruelty of humanity repeatedly, but in different disguises.

But right now, at this very moment, he was a man fighting for his life.

"Left!" Barry cried out.

Harry swept his gloved fist to the left and connected with the jaw of a Zom, a civilian wired electronically so that they no longer had free will but were robots...no longer able to resist the evil they were ordered to do. It sickened Harry, but he had to defend himself.

Then he saw whom he had struck.

A teenage girl, about five six, her fingernails long enough to act like knives and sharpened at the tips, just like daggers. The teeth in her mouth, of which he had just knocked several loose, were filed to points.

She screamed angrily, barely registering the pain of the blow, but enough to react.

He whirled around to grab her out reaching hands and jerks her past him.

Barry caught her by the waist, upended her and cracked the side of her skull with a hammer he had made just for this occasion.

Sparks flew and the girl fell to the ground at his feet, unconscious.

Harry didn't have time to see what happened next, he was grabbed by several Zoms at the same time as Barry was by one huge Zom, who must have been one helluva bruiser at one time.

The Zom stood at least seven feet tall, with bulging muscles that threatened to break away from the arms and chest that bore.

"Jesus!" Harry cried out.

But he was struck at that same moment of spotting the Bruiser by the other two Zoms.

He went down.

Barry screamed Harry's name, then went silent.

Doctor Zombie

"No!" The man pleaded.

He fell to his knees in front of the Swash that had been guarding him. The Swash was Nazi soldiers. The name was slang that their prisoners and the Allied Forces had given them. It was not meant to be a kind word. It embodied everything that a good soul despised!

Their faces were frozen in a perpetual scowl. Were they to think about what they were about to put this man through they would crack. And if they cracked, the madman who ran the factory would have them in his damned machine as well.

He was the UberDoctor. The man that Hitler used for all his dirty experiments. The ones that opponents in wars never talk about openly, because all sides do them in one way or another...just not so openly.

But these experiments went beyond testing a man or woman or child for their endurance or testing new drugs.

This experiment was the King of Experiments. It left the person subjected to it...different. Changed. Some said forever. But no one knew for certain. They only knew one thing they didn't want it to happen to them.

"NO!" The man screamed as the Doctor gestured to two Swash, who grabbed the man beneath his armpits and dragged him kicking and screaming into a huge tube filled with a vile smelling green gas. They immediately strapped him into it, first his legs, and then his arms and slammed the opening shut and double sealed it as instructed.

They stepped back, their gas masks still on.

The prisoners still waiting for their turn at the horrible machine smelled the vile gas, its odor violating their very soul with its pungent, sweet, but sickening smell.

Children began sobbing.

Their mothers gathered them close.

"It's all right. You're going to be all right, honey," they told them.

But they weren't going to be. No one would ever be all right after they were Zommed. A term for turning a human being into a living robot.

Doctor Zombie, as he was named, turned on his stunted leg to face the other prisoners, who were staring in a kind of dazed horror at the man now strapped in the green tube.

"You are so very welcome to witness the successful building of our Fuehrer's next generation of Zoms.

The Swash to the right and left stiffened. They had been told what a Zom was and the idea of it was horrifying to them; but the idea of disobeying this man was even worse.

Doctor Zombie was a short man. About five and a half feet tall. His right leg was stunted. Had been so from early childhood. It had grown equally with the other until he became five and then stopped growing as much.

His right leg was shorter than the left by almost a foot. He wore boots with lifters on the right one to help even out his height, but even with those he could barely walk properly.

When he walked his gait was like that of a penguin that had been wounded. He would step, drag, and then slide his right foot. Then repeat it again.

No one could ever miss this man, because of the sound that his dragging foot always made. The one with the lifts was made of metal so his foot had more support and didn't bend when his left leg weakened.

His head was bald.

Deliberately so.

It helped him frighten the prisoners more. The guards more yet. And even the Fuehrer, who never waited long to dismiss him because of the aura of the man.

When the darkest man of the Nazi Empire feared this man, it was more than reason enough for others to beware.

If Hitler feared the man to some degree, you could only imagine how much more so anyone else would. It was not his outer appearance so much that was frightening, but the psychic makeup of the man. His eyes lit with the fires of hell when he was angered and even when in a good mood, they seldom diminished to anything less than a raging fire of anger.

The man hated his life; hated the world; and most of all...hated Jews.

Even though his parents had been Jews, it made no difference. He damned them for bringing him into the world, twisted and broken. Unlike all the children he had grown up with, he was different from the start. Taking things more seriously. More personally.

Putting his nose in medical books when the other kids were just learning how to read literature books by the great men of the past. He was busy reading about the great men of the present...and the chemists.

He also, like Hitler, which also endeared him to the man who would rule the world, dabbled in the black arts. He believed the world was hollow and inhabited by fifteen-foot giants who hated humanity. He, just like Hitler, hoped one day to meet them and compare notes, never once believing that they, themselves, might be seen by the Hollow Earth giants in the same way as the Nazis saw the Jewish race....as something to despise and eradicate.

But such is the weakness of minds driven by evil and darkness. They never see the light in anything else, but themselves, and that light is murky at best because it is not based on the love of life, but rather its opposite, an appalling hatred for self and life.

Doctor Zombie narrowed his pale blue eyes, which always looked like watered down watercolors that had drained into a base of water tainted with oils. He gestured with a right forefinger that wore the symbol of Loch on it.

Loch was the cult that Doctor Zombie captained when he was not busy with his experiments. Even Hitler knew nothing of them. And that could one day spell trouble for both men, but for now the Doctor kept his affiliations to himself and his covert activities highly secret.

"See to him!" He ordered.

The Swash at the controls of the Zom Machine nodded, saluted, "Heil Hitler!"

Then the Swash turned smartly to his right, clasped the handle of the huge machine next to him and threw it down.

Base

"I'm telling you it's him," Harry told Al, which was short for Albert Einstein, his mentor, and the man who had helped him keep his sanity through all the changes he had gone through and continued to go through.

He was an anchor in the darkness of a battlefield that went far beyond fighting Nazis, but also in fighting for his sanity.

Captain Harry Morgan sprawled across the simple chair in front of Al's desk and gestured with his right forefinger at the map on the wall to the right of Al.

Al turned to look at it. His bushy brown hair was starting to turn gray at the temples and streaks were appearing in his locks as well, which he studiously tried to keep as hidden as possible.

Harry grinned at that thought. Everyone was so stuck on the man's genius; they never saw his frailties, his fallibilities, and his humanity. Harry did. He saw it every day.

From the man's aversion to anything chocolate. Reminded him of Switzerland and its pact with the Nazis to remain free.

Mozart. "German!" Al always exclaimed.

Beethoven. "German!" Again, Al exclaimed.

"Well, what do you like then?" Harry had asked one day after turning off his record player yet again so Al wouldn't go ballistic on him.

Al brought his hands from behind his back and smiled.

So now, Harry and Al were listening to Jimmy Dorsey and his band, while discussing World War Three and the end of World War Two.

"You tried hard to stop him, you know," Al told him, his eyes on Harry's. "But you failed."

Harry shrugged. "A man can only do so much. He was just too prepared. I can't stop Goons now without a big gun or a lot of luck. But to have to fight off a whole squad of them single handed. Nope. Not likely. Forget that, Pops. Just can't be done."

Al winced.

He hated being called Pops.

"I am not your Pop."

"Okay, Old Man," Harry corrected, knowing that would just infuriate him further.

Al started to go after Harry, but then he caught himself. Then his eyes narrowed, and he leaned forward on his desk to examine Harry's face more closely. "You're playing with me."

"Not."

"You are."

"Am not."

"Captain Harry Morgan, I am not an old fool; nor am I a young one. Well not so young, but not so old either. But a fool in neither one of those cases. You are up to something, and I want to know what?"

Harry just smiled.

Hug Love

Betty took one look at Harry's wound and tears flowed from her eyes. "Damnit, Harry!"

He sat there calmly on the doctor's examination table, legs crossed below it, wiggling them back and forth like a child...which he felt like at that moment and loving every moment of it.

"What's wrong?" He asked innocently.

"You bastard!" She cursed him. "This is festering."

He shrugged. "Just another day in the life of..."

She slugged him hard on his other shoulder.

He laughed.

Then she slugged him hard on his wounded one.

He let out a yelp like a dog that had been kicked.

"Hey!" He warned her.

"Don't hey me! That shouldn't have hurt that much if it's not such a big thing," she warned him and then shoved him hard down on the table, and hurriedly began strapping him down.

"What are you doing?" He asked.

She just smiled.

Fallen

Harry flipped himself over in a short acrobatic leap he had learned from gymnastics during training. Normally, you'd only do this to the other guy, but sometimes a hard choice required a little innovation.

As he flipped, the arms gripping him were twisted so hard that the two Zoms who had grabbed him unexpectedly were thrown from their feet.

Harry landed between them.

Reluctantly he kicked first one, then the other in their control boxes.

Sparks flew.

The two men, both in their late forties, spasmed several times and then lay limp.

Harry immediately spun about to help Barry.

Barry was on the shoulders of the Bruiser, struggling to power force the control pack from the lug's skull. But it wouldn't budge. And the Bruiser was pounding the heck out of Barry, even if he was on his back.

"Use your hammer, you idiot!" Harry hollered.

Barry held up a broken hammer handle.

"Oh!" Harry muttered.

Without pausing to think he rushed the monster of a Zom and kicked him right in the breadbasket.

The Bruiser just looked at Harry.

"Damn!" Harry cursed.

"Got that right!" Barry told him just before the Bruiser reached over his shoulder and tossed Barry into Harry.

Friendship's Course

H arry continued to look straight into Al's eyes calmly. "Nothing."
Al leaned forward, his eyes blazing with anger.

"Damnit it all, Harry, you're not just an experiment; you're my friend! Tell me what's going on?"

Harry gave the old man a surprised look. "You just swore at me."

"No, I didn't," Al protested.

"Yes, you did," Harry insisted.

"I never swear."

"Sure, sounded like one to me," Harry insisted.

Al shook his head. "You're impossible. Get out of my sight!"

Harry jumped to his feet and saluted Al. "Sure thing, Pops."

Harry made it out the office door, just before something big slammed into it.

He grinned.

Sky Captain

Harry whistled happily as he cleaned and polished up his battle-scarred Sky Captain suit.

First, he hand burnished the helmet, making sure the visor was so clean you could see perfectly through it from the inside and the outside. He spotted a bubble of dirt in the right corner of the visor, spit on it and cleaned it off, then began rubbing down the metal section, carefully avoiding the fine printed circuits embedded on the inside as he cleaned that as well.

The inside of the helmet was a work of art. State of the art microphone and receiver embedded just below the visor, tactical screens, and power controls just above the visor.

All perfectly placed to give him one heck of a headache once he plucked the helmet from over his head and set it aside.

Least he didn't have to use his tongue anymore to activate the controls. He almost wanted to spit to get that bitter metal taste out of his mouth...and that was just from the memories of all the times he had to do that.

No, the controls were all voice activated.

He had Tesla and Edison to thank for that. They had worked together hard for months to perfect the science.

When two geniuses get together miracles happen and when they have Zoms, Swash and nuclear weapons eating at their butts, miracles happen even faster yet.

Satisfied everything was clean he made a mental note for Edison to find someone who could pad the interior of the helmet to make it more soundproof. The last bomb that had gone off near his helmet had made him deaf for hours afterwards. He couldn't afford to lose his hearing.

Fortunately, he was used to taking a pounding like that and had learned how to speak to the deaf and dumb, so when worst came to worst he could hand signal, but that was a bit hard to do inside your helmet when you were flying and there was no two way screen for the other side...Base...to know just what the hell you were doing, let alone signaling, even if they could have seen outside the helmet somehow.

He sighed happily, not the least bit annoyed at the complications of his life at that moment, just meandering through random memories to pass the time while he did his maintenance.

Finished with the helmet, he hung it back up and then began working on his boots and shoes. He wore boots sometimes, especially when he was doing the high altitude flying and shoes when it was mostly air to ground no more than several thousand feet.

The boots were helpful. They served a dual purpose. Because they were oversized, Al and Tes...Harry's nickname for Tesla...had managed to squeeze a miniature rocket launcher in his right and left boots. Woe to anyone who got in his face, or in this case, his backside when he was wearing these babies...because he could launch a pair of deadly rockets into their faces!

He carefully ministered to the boots, making sure the loading mechanism was clean and no rust was building up. He carefully reclosed the rocket port, and then did a test of the firing electronics. They lit up green on the right boot and then the left. He hung them up next to his helmet and then took down his rocket backpack.

The rocket tubes were bright and golden copper colored. The exhaust ports were smudged from heat exhaust and moisture, so he took out a scrub brush and began working on those. Didn't want to find out his rockets failed because they fell apart.

If they were going to do that, better it happen now when he could repair them. Once he had launched into the air, he had one chance in a million of surviving a catastrophic failure. And he didn't want to bet on his surviving it.

After several more hours of scrubbing, mending, rubbing, waxing, polishing, testing, and making sure everything was snug as could be, he was finally able to give his mind over to what Al wanted to know, but he wasn't going to tell until it was too late to stop him.

Harry was a good American. He believed in chain of command. He believed in taking orders, to doing the right thing. But he didn't believe in leaving friends behind. Even if they were from another time and not the same one.

Even if he didn't have a clue in hell of how close they were in this life, or if at all. No, he was doing it because it was the right thing to do. And sooner than later, he knew he'd be expanding to the other prisoners as well.

He eyed the holster racked on the wall next to his backpack, helmet, boots, pants, and jacket. But next to the holster on its other side, he eyed the weapon that was framed there behind glass, with a note reading, "Break in case of emergency."

He smiled.

It was Barry's sense of humor he had found out from a friendly grunt stationed near his barracks.

The weapon was untried.

Al had said it was particularly destructive and not to use it unless he felt he had a dire need.

He eyed the weapon thoughtfully.

Hank

"Hey Harry!" Hank greeted as Harry climbed onto his bunk to take a rest.

It had been a hard night. The Base alarms had gone off repeatedly, making everyone think they had finally been discovered. A fear that undermined every day's work and everyone's thoughts.

The Swiss couldn't be trusted to know about them, so even those Base workers who occasionally slipped into the town below, were careful not to ID themselves, for fear of exposing the Base.

Fortunately, the Allied Forces had planted agents in the towns of Switzerland that were friendly to the Base personnel and didn't expose them when they came for supplies, but instead greeted them normally as if they had known them all their lives.

And yes, they were Swiss as well. So not all Swiss were bad; just mostly scared for their lives.

Harry couldn't blame them for that. The things that Hitler's regime did to his own people, let along the ones he conquered were unthinkably dark and horrible.

But there was a dark side to the Swiss people as well. Some, high up in government, to protect their lives and families had agreed to co-operate with the Fourth Reich.

The town was rife with Nazi collaborators. Hitler, while honoring Switzerland's so-called neutrality, had secretly promised them safety only if they let him have his way with their people...covertly of course.

How the government managed to hide the fact that many of their most intelligent leaders and scientists were vanishing overnight, Harry didn't know.

He only knew they were, and so did the citizens, though none vocalized it for fear of vanishing themselves.

He was sure of one thing though, if the Swiss knew which leaders were betraying them, those leaders would probably vanish in the middle of the night too...peace loving nation or not!

Hank sprawled across his top bunk, his too long legs hanging over the end. Fortunately, no one slept beneath him, or they would have gotten a full whiff of his naked feet. Even from where Harry was, they stank.

"Native problem," Hank had told Harry once about his feet. "I sweat too much."

Hank had laughed, but Harry had let it go.

He had gotten used to the guys in his barracks and didn't complain. He had a roof, square meals, his body worked just fine, and he had plenty of work on duty and off to keep him busy and his mind occupied.

Off duty he made it a point to read up on how this current timeline differed from his original one. On duty he kicked Nazi butt. Swash and Goon. Though Goon not so much. They were getting bigger and bigger and the risk of confronting one who would plant a deadly blow to his backpack and hammer him to death were growing riskier.

But Harry was not one to frighten easily. Or give up.

"The bigger they are, the harder they fall!" He had told Hank one night when both couldn't sleep.

The snores of the other men didn't bother them. Their chatting didn't bother the sleepers either. No one ever got as much sleep as they wanted. It was wartime. No one slept comfortably forever. And no one ever slept for very long.

Unless they were dead.

"Ever heard of a flyboy named Barry?" Harry had asked out of the blue one night.

He had to speak up. Since he had left Barry after his last mission, his conscience had been troubling him. And he was close to making a decision that could change his life forever.

Hank had rolled over, curled into almost a fetal position so he could turn on his side on the too small bunk. He picked at his right nostril a moment in thought. A nervous habit that had begun in combat when he was a foot soldier and hadn't yet been drafted into the secret Base according to Hank.

Harry thought it more likely the man just never held back anything, filtered anything he did. Like a lot of older people did. Not caring anymore what people thought.

"Man, was he ever one cookie!"

Harry sat up. Expectant and hopeful.

"You knew him?"

Hank sat up too, climbed down and eyed Harry. Harry moved over so Hank could sit on his bunk. It lowered a couple inches from his weight. The man was muscled like a bulldozer, solid weight. Heavy.

"He and I used to joke all night long in the trenches."

"So, he wasn't a flyboy?"

Hank patted Harry on his head, like he might a dog and grinned. "Harry, the only boys flying after Hitler nuked the hell outta the world, were Japs."

Harry waited.

"And of course, once Hitler had American groveling at his feet, the Japs were no longer needed. As was Japan."

"What happened?"

"He used Japan to test out his next super weapon...something that begins with an H...oh yeah; he called it a hell bomb...powered by hydrogen or something."

"To the island?" Harry asked.

"Yeah, the whole flocking island went up in a cloud of smoke. Sent tsunamis around the world, crushed even more port cities than Hitler's nukes had during the first strike of the war. It was horrible."

Hank was quiet for a moment.

"There are no more Japanese?"

Hank shook his head. "There is no more Japanese nation, but the remainder has sworn allegiance to Hitler in the hopes of one day being able to rebuild their nation."

Hank spit onto the floor. "Good luck with that idea. Idiots."

Harry investigated Hank's face.

Hank wiped a tear away.

"Sorry, Harry. I don't mean to be down on them so much. Not all Germans are bad. Certainly not all Japanese either. But my mother was Japanese. She still lived there. In Tokyo. My father couldn't get her back to the states in time once the war began."

Hank looked into Harry's eyes.

"When news came that the Japan had been nuked into oblivion my father and I took it hard. Really hard."

Hank sighed deeply and wiped at his eyes again. Then he brightened.

"Barry was the man who got me out of my darker days. His jokes were more valuable to me than a million bucks, or one gorgeous blonde in high heels."

Hank thought about that a moment and grinned. "Well, maybe not the blonde part, but the other, yeah. Totally."

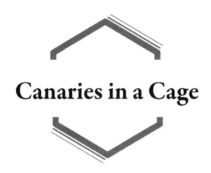

Canaries in a Cage

Harry struggled against the maglocks that kept him chained to the wall. Barry watched him from across the cell, straining against his own as well. Finally, they both stopped.

"Well if that doesn't take the cake." Barry finally said in a blast of exhaustion and frustration. "Stuck like canaries in a cage."

"Unfortunately, not likely to be kept alive for long," Harry pointed out.

"You think?" Barry replied with a curl of his lips. "This Doctor Zombie is not your average Japanese torturer, not even Nazi. He has a reputation for the finer points of murder...in slow, slow ways."

Both men had been strung up to the wall now for two days without food or water. Their pants were soiled and stinking and their arms hurt like hell as well. Their wrists and hands were going numb. Their legs were about to buckle, which meant they would probably collapse, causing their wrists to dislocate and the loss of both hands.

"Yeah. War stinks." Harry cursed. "And so, do we?"

"Well, the way I see it, pal, is that if the Nazis don't turn us into Zombies to kill our friends, then these Eastern Faction crazies going to rip our skin off to see what makes us tick."

"Eastern Faction?"

"What Doctor Zombie calls his allies. Don't let him know I know that. I overheard him talking to his allies when he thought no one was listening."

Harry considered that new information.

"Then there are dissenters among Hitler's ranks?"

"Big time. Always some jerk that thinks he can do it better..."

Barry grimaced and wiggled a bit, trying to get more comfortable. "Or in this case...worse."

"For us in both cases." Harry added.

"You had to say that didn't you? Didn't you?" Barry shot back.

"Hey! Someone's gotta keep up our spirits!"

"War is still hell."

"And it stinks!" Harry said sniffing the air in a comical manner.

"Now, now Harry. Just look at it as a little manly fragrance to pass the time away with."

"This is serious." Harry insisted.

"And it's never not been?"

"Noted."

"You should never have come back for me," Barry told Harry suddenly.

Harry eyed the scar where the control box had been on Barry's skull.

"Says who?"

"Me, you big lug!" Barry cursed. "I was just fine before you rocketed back into my life with that glory hound rocket suit of yours that sparkles like a cheap fake diamond in a jewelry store."

Harry laughed.

"What's so funny?"

"I had to piss off my best friend at Base to come here for you and what thanks do I get...you hate me!"

Barry suddenly looked away. He shook his head.

"I'm a guy. I say guy things. Don't mean I mean them."

Harry laughed again.

"What's so damned funny now?"

Harry smiled at Barry, who looked into his eyes again. "You remind me so much of my friend back home."

"Which home?"

Harry shrugged. "I'm not so sure anymore. I've been thrust into so many alternate timelines; I'm starting to get blurred memories."

"Sure, you haven't been doing too much whiskey?"

Harry laughed. "From where?"

Barry shrugged. "Well, there used to be. Good. Damn stuff's no good for you anyway."

Harry smiled. "Wouldn't know. Never drank it."

Barry eyed Harry. "Really, not even a taste?"

Harry thought back to his preteen years. "My brother and I snuck out behind our barn to try some. Made us both sicker than dogs. I never tried it again after that."

Barry laughed. Then he shut his eyes.

"Wish I could rub my head."

"Why?"

"Hurts."

"Why?"

Barry eyed Harry sternly. "You didn't have to hit that damned control box so hard. You know my skull was attached to it!"

Harry smiled. "Now there's the Barry I knew and loved."

"Not in this world, flyboy. Not in this world. In this world I am one mean sonuvabitch and I eat Swash for breakfast."

Both men broke into laughter, then lapsed into a lingering silence.

Finally, Harry sighed, and then looked to the solid wall that opened to allow their captors inside. "What do you think they want from us?"

"Maybe a malted chocolate and fries."

Harry laughed despite himself. "Barry!"

"Yeah man. Thinking. Thinking." Shakes his head. "Nope. No idea. You?"

Then the wall opened, making an ominous hissing sound as it did so.

Nurse Death

Before Harry could reply, the door in the wall slid open, revealing a very beautiful oriental woman clad in a doctor's smock. Her hands were covered in gloves.

"This don't look good, Harry." Barry said, eyeing the gloves.

"Losing your touch with the ladies, Barry?"

"In this case I'll make an exception." Barry quipped, again his eyes not leaving those gloved hands. Finally, he looked up. "I hope those gloves have got useful purposes...like letting us out of our prison, feeding us, arming us."

The oriental woman neither smiled, nor responded. She came into the room, plucked a thermometer from her smock, stuck it in Harry's mouth, then went to the other side of the room and did the same with Barry.

Barry smiled at her. "My favorite flavor. None. And thanks for just using my oral cavity. Much appreciated."

Her eyes flickered for a moment in surprise. She even looked like she might smile, but she managed to control her facial expression and she said nothing. She left the room.

Harry looked over at Barry. "I think your charm is making headway."

"Yeah. Like an airplane crash."

They both laughed.

Several minutes later the door opened again, and the same oriental woman entered the room, plucked the thermometers out, made a note of their temperatures, and then exited again.

She looked back once at Barry, then smiled.

"What the hell?" Barry asked no one in particular. "She really hates me, this Nurse Death."

"Don't be so quick to judge her, Barry."

"I'm not. I'm talking strictly about my chances of a hot date. She just walked out on the only man who would make her sick, perverted life happy."

Harry laughed.

"Even if only for a night," Barry added with a grin.

Harry shook his head. "You're something else."

"I owe it all to you, Harry. Or at least the Harry I used to know. He was a lot like you, you know."

"I don't," Harry replied.

Barry smiled.

"Well, I have to admit, it does help pass the time between getting nowhere fast and possibly being tortured next," Harry said.

Barry perked up. "You think?"

Harry didn't respond. Suddenly, the gravity of their situation was coming back again. He had managed to muffle his emotions, but the stress of the waiting was getting to him.

He had taken several courses in what to do if captured and tortured and they always ended with the words, "Don't blame yourself if you break. Most men do!"

He didn't want to think about it. He knew what kind of tortures the Orientals on his own timeline had used during World War Two; he could only imagine what the ones in this crazy cocked up one would do. And judging just by the craziness he had already seen; it couldn't be very pretty at all.

The door opened again and then a short man in a doctor's smock entered. He was glancing at a notepad in his hands. He was escorted by what appeared to be Samurai, except that instead of swords they carried these wicked looking rods with barbed tips that emitted sparks every now and then.

What Harry noticed next was that the doctor dragged his right foot.

Barry swallowed. The torture was about to begin. He gave Harry a nod and Harry nodded back.

The large man gestured to Barry.

The guards headed for him.

"Harry!"

"Don't worry, pal. I'll be there for you when the time comes."

Barry looked back at Harry as he was removed from his maglocks. "You're kidding? Right? Right?"

The Doctor eyed Barry and motioned to the guards to stop a moment.

"I am Doctor Zombie. No one will be there for you when the time comes."

Barry snarled. "You don't look like a zombie!"

Doctor Zombie gave Barry a scathing glance. "You escaped my control once, but you will not be so lucky the next time."

He turned to Harry. "And you...you shouldn't make promises you can't keep."

"I don't," Harry snapped.

Doctor Zombie recoiled, stepping back a pace, almost falling, and if not for the quick reaction of one of the guards, who steadied him.

Doctor Zombie shook the guard's hand off, and then grunted at the guards.

He exited the room, dragging his right foot as he did so.

As the guards walked past Harry, he suddenly jerked his entire body upwards, straining against the maglocks holding his hands, and kicked the nearest Samurai Guard in his crotch.

The Samurai Guard froze a moment.

Barry and Harry waited.

The Samurai Guard slowly grinned, shook his head, and then wagged a finger at Harry like he was being a naughty, naughty boy.

He acted as if to reach for Barry, but instead swung around and shoved his rod at Harry, who managed to throw himself upwards so that his hands and their maglocks were in the way of his chest.

Sparks ignited from the metal.

Harry fell back with a loud cry of pain and slumped against the wall.

"Damn! Harry! Harry!" Barry cried. Barry broke free to reach Harry but was immediately stopped by a jab of the prod to his chest.

Barry screamed.

Harry didn't move.

The Samurai Guard gave Harry a second shock, this time to his chest, grinned broadly, then gestured to the other guard, who pushed the still struggling Barry, who was fighting the pain in his body from the electric shock still. The door irised shut after the men exited.

Harry's body hung on the maglocks for what seemed like forever, but then a strange thing occurred. He groaned as if in a lot of pain, but what made it so strange was when his eyes open and he smiled.

Doctor Zombie

Barry was hauled into a large warehouse with an open door at the opposite end, where Japanese Soldiers were marching. Rows of odd-looking tanks lined opposite walls. The tank cannons all appeared like the rods the guards carried. He was then marched to a large table where his and Harry's jump suits lay stretched out.

Doctor Zombie no wore a Nazi uniform jacket over his white doctor's outfit. A Swash symbol lit the shoulder of his right arm, showing a red skull with crossbones on it and a Nazi Swastika overlaying that. He looked up from the rocket suits.

"Ah, I see you have accepted our invitation to join us after all.

He nodded to the large man holding Barry's arms behind him and that man walked off. The two guards, who had marched to the left and right of Barry, touched his wrist maglocks and they fell off.

Barry immediately tensed as if to fight, but when the guards raised their weapons defensively, he thought better of it and instead fell to rubbing his wrists and hands to get the blood circulating again.

Later, he thought.

He grinned.

The guards and Doctor Zombie gave him surprised looks.

Doctor Zombie nodded to the guards, and they stepped aside, giving Barry more space.

Barry fixed a stare on Doctor Zombie's face. "I don't like your invitations."

"You're here, aren't you?"

"Did I have any other choice?"

"To die."

"Fair enough," Barry said. "Have it your way."

"Come now. Surely you can appreciate a bit of humor considering what we could alternatively choose to do?"

"You mean like hanging me on a wall and torturing me?"

"Oh no, that would be too uncivilized."

Doctor Zombie gestured to the right and then Barry saw the silent men and women in uniform that stood at perfect attention. Their faces rigid and immobile, fists clenched against their hips. They wore Nazi armbands.

"Zombies!" Barry uttered, the horror of what he was seeing gripping his heart and soul. "Nazi Zombies."

Barry gave the scientist an ugly scowl. "Even your own men? You do this to even your own people?"

"They are not my people!" Doctor Zombie said, his voice barely above a whisper, but fraught with emotion.

Then he shrugged. "Germans, Japanese, Americans. What's the difference? Cattle are cattle. I'm sure you understand."

"What I understand is that you have no heart," Barry shot back.

"Ah, but that presumes I ever had one."

Doctor Zombie pulled back the cloth from his chest and revealed slight scars in a box shape. He carefully pried on the right edge, and it opened to reveal mechanical and electrical pumps and engines. Sparks flew from one circuit to the next.

Where the heart should have been was a huge device shaped like a heart, with multiple pump lines attached to it. It didn't expand and contract.

What did were two bladders just below the heart. They did.

Doctor Zombie smiled. "You see how simple, yet how complex I am. My blood...such as it is...is pumped by the device just above the two bladders, which serve as lungs for me."

"How could you do this to yourself?" Barry hissed in horror.

Doctor Zombie reclosed his chest. "I had no choice. Just as you now have no choice."

He leaned closer, looking up into Barry's face. "Choices are for men who have freewill. Not such as you or I."

Barry shook his head.

"I don't believe you. We always have a choice."

Doctor Zombie smiled.

The smile filled Barry with a sudden horror. He didn't know why.

He felt his right hand begin to shake, then his left.

"You assume so much for a creation."

Barry began shaking in his left hand next.

He felt his heartbeat accelerating.

Barry looked on in horror.

"Creation? What are you talking about? I'm a human being!"

Doctor Zombie came closer to Barry and looked into his eyes. "Do you not recognize the one who made you?"

Barry's horror grew even more.

He began spasming as shocking memories began colliding in the back of his mind.

He couldn't move.

Then he let out a scream.

Again, and again and again.

The Zombie Machine

Barry strained to break free from the muscle men of Doctor Zombie as other horrified prisoners looked on, moaning, or muttering in terror.

Swash had them all under control, their weapons aimed for any who might choose a swift death, rather than being turned into a Zom, a zombie.

Doctor Zombie smiled at Barry. "I like you, Barry. You show more promise than the rest. Swear allegiance to me now and I will spare you the humiliation of becoming a living robot, able to witness and experience all the horrors inflicted upon you or you inflict upon others."

"Never!" Barry responded, his blood boiling with anger.

Doctor Zombie stepped closer.

Barry tried to break free from the Swash restraining him; but it was no use; he was immobilized.

"You struggle, even knowing it would cause you death if you somehow managed to break free?"

Barry gave Doctor Zombie a look of utter contempt. "Does it matter? Does it really, really matter which way I die?"

"You contemptible fool!" Doctor Zombie snarled at Barry. "I can offer you immortality!"

Doctor Zombie opened his chest to reveal his mechanical innards.

Barry recoiled in horror.

"You understand now?"

Barry shook his head over and over.

"I can never die. If a part breaks, it only need be replaced and I'm good as new."

"No," Barry uttered.

"Join me, Barry. You will become immortal. Be what God has meant you to become. Not a slave, but a master of life!"

"Never!"

Doctor Zombie sighed, then nodded to the Swash holding Barry and they rushed him towards the huge cylinder with swirls of green gas inside.

Doctor Zombie

Every muscle in his body was spasming, but he couldn't move. Finally, the series of visions blew away as if a powerful wind had blown away clouds. His eyes cleared and he stared into Doctor Zombie's face. His face was like stone.

"You should never have done that to me. To anyone."

"But I did. I have and I will so again," Doctor Zombie assured Barry. "You see, I share the Fuehrer's vision of the future. A state where the few rules and the rest are just part of the machinery that operates it. Even become part machinery. Like me."

He grinned.

Barry felt sick to his stomach at what he saw in the man's face.

"A state of absolute obedience!"

Doctor Zombie snickered. "And you could have become a leader. A man above the rest. Now you shall become even less than the Zoms. A hollow man with no feelings whatsoever."

Barry managed to shake off both his guards for a moment as he rushed the Doctor, but their reactions were faster than his and they snapped him back against them again, locking their hand tightly about his arms.

The Doctor smiled. Their grips relaxed.

Barry tensed, ready to spring again for the Doctor, but the guards felt his tension and tightened their grip again.

Doctor Zombie stepped so close that Barry could hear the machinery operating in his chest.

"I have never forgotten you, Barry. You always were the one that got away. Both figuratively and literally in the end. I look forward to inspecting your brain to see how that happened."

Barry gave him a surprised look. "I thought you wanted to make me a Zom again?"

"Oh, I want much more than that."

Doctor Zombie clapped his hands.

Barry used that moment to try and break free again, but it was useless. The guards tightened their grip so hard; he could feel his bones threatening to crack.

He yelped in pain.

"Good!' Doctor Zombie said with a smile. "You see now how useless it is to resist."

Doctor Zombie thumped a hand against the head of the nearest guard, and it rang like a bell. The guard flinched, but didn't lose his grip on Barry, who was stunned.

"They're robots!"

"True robots. Surely, you didn't think ordinary Swash could hold you, did you?"

"You're mad." Barry swore. "No good will ever come of this!"

"Oh, but it already has. I expect you to talk excitedly about these..." He pointed to the jump suits. "And very loudly."

One of the guards quite unexpectedly broke Barry's left pinkie.

Barry screamed in pain.

"Am I making myself quite clear, Barry? Because if you do not talk; if you do not serve me, then you shall become like my men. Hollow!"

"But how, how did he know to..." Barry uttered despite his growing pain. How had the guard known to break his finger? The Doctor hadn't even so much as glanced at the man, let alone made a gesture.

The scientist tapped his head. "Here. I have found a way to connect myself to all my creations."

And upon those words every single zombie in the lineups turned and saluted Doctor Zombie, stomping on the floor in time to a Nazi goosestep to boot.

"Damn!" Barry muttered, a smile coming to his lips. "Busby Berkeley could sure use these guys!"

Barry screamed even louder when his right pinkie was broken.

"What the hell you do that for, man?" Barry hollered. Hot tears of pain and frustration were pouring from his eyes now. He couldn't help it. It hurt!

Doctor Zombie tapped his head. "Because I can. Now, shall we talk as peace loving men, or shall we continue our little game of sticks and stones. And prove just how frail your human body is."

Doctor Zombie started to smile and then grimaced and made a very, very ugly face as his forehead sprouted a blossom of red. He tumbled to the concrete floor and lay there unmoving.

Barry broke away from the guards, expecting them to stop him, but they were frozen in place. Alarms began to ring.

Harry came running from behind a tank, tossing a Japanese rifle to the ground as he dashed Barry's way. "Suit up!" He screamed.

Barry turned to follow Harry, but before he got one foot away, Doctor Zombie's left hand reached out and grabbed his right ankle.

"God!" Screamed Barry.

Harry turned around just as Doctor Zombie began to sit up and all the robot guards and zombies began to stir.

"Not his head, Harry!" Barry hollered, struggling to break free.

Harry didn't ask why. He just grabbed the rifle from the nearest robot Swash, and then rushed Doctor Zombie with the bayonet on its barrel.

"Noooo!" Doctor Zombie screamed, as Harry stabbed the bayonet into where the heart should have been and repeatedly fired the rifle.

Each time he fired, the Doctor spasmed and all the Zoms and robots spasmed as well.

Harry let go the rifle.

"Where in the world did you get that rifle, Harry?" Barry demanded.

"This cute oriental nurse gave it to me after she clobbered the guard of my cell."

Barry grinned broadly. "I knew she thought I was hot!"

Doctor Zombie twitched on the floor a long time, and then slowly, slowly, slowly began to sit up. He smiled. A smile that was so hideous and terrible that both Barry and Harry grimaced in horror.

"I cannot die; I am immortal," Doctor Zombie exclaimed with a hideous smile.

"Suit up!" Harry warned Barry.

"And just when I was getting ready to go back and grab a quick goodbye," Barry joked.

Harry ran for his suit and began scrambling into it.

Barry lagged.

When Harry turned around, finally in his suit, Barry grinned.

"What's the grin for?"

"Oh, just a little something I left for the good doctor," Barry explained as he hurried into his own rocket suit.

They both turned to look.

Doctor Zombie had a dozen hand grenades wrapped around him, pins ready to pop off if he moved.

"I never taught you to do that," Harry scolded Barry.

Barry grinned. "Papa doesn't know everything," he said with a grin.

Then he began running for the massive doors that opened into the bunker they were in.

He struck a huge button on the way and the massive doors began to widen slowly. Slowly.

Harry followed closely.

A barrage of bullets began following them as the robot Swash recovered enough to take orders from Doctor Zombie, who was still rising, but slowly, slowly.

Even as he rose his chest began to seal up, his face to mend.

"Stop them! Stop them!" Doctor Zombie hollered.

"Rockets away!" Harry hollered.

"You got it!" Barry cried out.

Both men leaped into the air and their rockets cut in and propelled them towards the massive doors, which were now beginning to close.

"Damn!" Harry cursed.

Barry joined him. "Double damn!"

Swash appeared outside the closing doors.

"Ever had a close shave before, Barry."

"Yeah...every day with you!" Barry cursed.

"I thought you were never with me," Harry accused.

"Might as well have been!" Harry snarled.

"Then trust me, it's going to get scary. Follow me!" Harry ordered.

"In case you're not looking, I already am," Barry roared from his position to the right of Harry.

Then Harry turned totally sideways and accelerated.

Barry followed suit. "You're crazy!"

"Better crazy than dead," Harry promised.

Then both men shot out the closing door, just an inch on both sides of them from being smashed to atoms.

The doors smashed shut behind them and the bullets from inside stopped, but now the Swash outside the bunker turned their weapons on them, spinning around to track and fire upon them.

"Ow!" Barry cried out as they shot over the encampment and the vast warehouse, they had been held captive in.

"Where you shot, Barry?"

"I'm not! My damn pinkies, they're both broken, and I forgot that and tried to use them."

"Next time, use your middle finger." Harry joked.

Barry did. But not on his controls.

The two rocket men shot upwards and safely into the high clouds overhead.

Base

The crew in the hanger of the base all applauded and cheered as Harry and Barry landed safely on their feet in the middle of the concrete bull's eye made for Harry.

Harry took his helmet off immediately and turned to help Barry, but before he could finish turning, he was enveloped in a huge hug.

Barry held him like a Teddy Bear in his arms and kissed him on both cheeks. "Man, if you were a woman, I'd marry you right about now."

Harry shoved Barry back. "Hey!"

Barry then remembered they weren't alone. The whole hanger was filled, and everyone was watching the two of them.

He grinned and put a hand in the air. "Hi everyone!"

The applause broke out again.

Hank came running up. "Barry!"

"Hey man!" Barry cried out and ran to Hank and gave him a big hug.

"Hey, don't I get a kiss too, little buddy?" Hank demanded with a grin.

Barry grinned back. "Kiss of my right fist maybe."

Hank gave him a hug back and turned to Harry, who joined them. "A tornado is on its way."

Harry gave him a blank look.

"You disobeyed a direct command, abandoned your post and risked exposing the entire Base!" Al exclaimed as he rushed towards Harry and Barry.

"Me too?" Barry asked.

Al looked at Barry a moment, nodded, and then put his attention fully on Harry again. "What do you have to say for yourself, young man?"

"It's good to be home again," Harry said after a long pause.

The hanger became so quiet you could hear a pin drop.

Harry gave Al a sad look. "I guess its back to loading crates and greasing wheels again then."

Al gave Harry a scowl. "It sure as hell..."

Then he broke into a big grin. Hollered. "Isn't!"

The hanger cleared a bit, and the Base Cook came forward, along with several helpers, with carts loaded with cake and drinks.

In moments the food and drink was dispensed to everyone, and some music was turned on and men and women began dancing with each other.

Overlooking the Lake

"It's freezing, Harry!" Betty complained.

Harry, who had fallen asleep with his head on her lap, rubbed his eyes and sat up. He immediately took off his jacket and draped it around her shoulders.

He pulled her against him, and they watched the city below with its twinkling lights.

"You did a good thing today, Harry."

Harry was silent.

She turned to look into his eyes. "But I could have lost you."

Harry stayed silent.

"Say something, Damnit!" She cursed.

Harry laughed.

She pulled away and banged his shoulder with her fist.

"Wrong shoulder," he told her.

She laughed and he pulled her into a kiss.

When both felt as if they might faint from lack of oxygen, they pulled away.

"We didn't get him," Harry said finally.

Betty gave him a questioning look.

"You got him. Barry's safe. You brought him back. I saw him myself."

"No! Not him; Doctor Zombie."

Betty shivered even more strongly this time.

Harry didn't try to warm her. He knew it wasn't from the cold.

"You're going back, aren't you?" She asked, even though it was more of an accusation.

He looked into her eyes. "I don't want to lose you."

"Likewise, you big goof!" She told him.

"You mean a lot to me," he told her.

"And you mean a lot to me," she assured him.

Then he looked out over the lake again. "But I've got to go back. First, it was to free Barry, but now it's to free them all."

"You're just one man, Harry. You got lucky this time. Maybe not the next."

Harry didn't hear those words. He just said in a very firm tone, "I won't rest until they're all free!"

Betty shivered again and he pulled her closer.

They both jerked away when they heard a loud crunching sound nearby.

Harry reached for his sidearm.

A hand caught his wrist.

"You wouldn't shoot your best buddy now, would you?"

Harry smiled.

Barry let go and sat between Harry and Betty, who scooted over to make room. Barry put his arms around both and pulled them back, against him. "Now this is what I call comfy."

Betty and Harry broke into laughter.

And a moment later a sharp ball of light thrust across the skies, a blazing trail hurling behind it.

Harry's eyes narrowed.

"Another weapon of mass destruction. Won't they ever stop?"

Barry sighed. He looked at Harry. "Probably not. But we can't let that ruin our evening together, can we?"

"What kind of weapon do you think it was?" Harry asked.

Barry shook his head. "Deadly."

Harry sighed.

The three lapsed into a depressed silence, but then the hint of music grew from above them at the Base's entrance. It grew louder and louder.

They turned about to look.

Behind them, standing in the opening to the secret base were all the men and women from the base. And they were singing a song that Harry didn't realize existed on this world, or maybe it hadn't. But it did now.

He looked at Barry, who shrugged, but then gave him a wink.

It was a song that he remembered well from his childhood, something that meant everything wonderful and good in the world was coming, that the entire world was at peace.

A Christmas song.

And a simple one.

He broke into laughter.

"Damnit it all, Harry; Betty and I stayed up all night teaching them that song for you! What the hell's so funny about it?"

Harry kept laughing.

Barry and Betty gave him a weird look, and then they realized he wasn't laughing at them.

He was laughing at the universe and how no matter where you were, that somehow it all fit together and somehow it was all right.

He wiped at the tears in his eyes and gave them both a hug.

"Thank you!" He choked out.

"For what?" Barry asked.

"For being you," Harry replied.

"Now you can kiss me," Barry sighed, making eyes at Harry.

Harry slugged him.

Barry and Harry broke into laughs.

Betty gave them both hugs and kisses, then hauled them to their feet to join in the singing, which was an old traditional Christmas song, "Silent Night!"

And what made it even the stranger for Harry not just the fact that this world was singing his song, but that now at the same moment the first flakes of snow began to fall on his and his friend's shoulders.

Harry smiled happily, but then he noticed Barry wasn't.

"What's wrong, Barry?"

"Nurse Death," Barry sighed.

Harry thought back to what she had done.

He put a hand on Barry's shoulder.

"You up for another mission, buddy?"

Barry brightened.

DOCTOR ZOMBIE

Mather Air Force Base

Commissary
Sacramento, California
Night

Chuck Bassett sat down at the back of the commissary a moment to rest. He had been cleaning up for hours now. His shift began at Midnight, when all the regulars left and military staff.

The commissary was a pitiful one by comparison to a grocery story, but it got the job done. Pickles. Vinegar. Coffee. Sodas. Candy bars. It had all the essentials that an air force team and their families needed to survive without having to leave the base.

Most chose to do both. Food here was cheap, but it was the same all the time. The big superstores in Civvie country were stocked with ever changing brands. He couldn't remember a store he had visited that didn't have at least forty different brands of coffee and a hundred different kinds of candy bars.

Here luck was to have four or five brands of coffee, usually the cheaper; and the standard candies like Hershey and Mars Bars.

Not that he didn't like them; he just didn't find them fitting his taste. He was more of a peanut butter kind of guy, so Reese's pieces were his thing.

He looked at the mop and bucket seated on the floor between his legs and frowned. Best he could hope for at this point in his life. On his miserable salary he couldn't even afford a hooker to get between his legs.

He burst into laughter. What a jerk he was he thought. Not that I could care that much. If I wanted to be with a doll, I could hit the clubs. Not worth it. After two wives and about twenty odd girlfriends he was close to becoming a confirmed bachelor.

Then his self-dissatisfaction and grumbling were whisked away by the sounds of sirens.

"What the hell?" He cursed as he jumped to his feet.

The sound of thunder in the distance.

He froze.

Thunder.

During the summer?

He knocked over the bucket of water as he leaped past it, stumbled several paces, taking down a shelving unit filled with soft toys, then scrambled for the front of the commissary. The only place where there were any windows.

As he ran the dark front of the commissary lit up brighter than the sun a moment. He flung his forearm to shield his eyes but kept running.

He reached the front of the building, ran past the cash registers, and stopped in front of the carts, staring off into the distance where Sacramento was. The state capitol of California.

A huge mushroom cloud of burning orange and yellow gasses streaked with fire the color of blood rose majestically into the sky.

"Oh shit!" He cursed.

Then the glass shattered into him, puncturing his body in a thousand places, and a second searing light flooded the commissary. What had not been shredded by the exploding glass was burned to a crisp by the heat wave that had followed.

End of the World

Commissary
Sacramento, California
Night

Chuck couldn't believe his eyes.

He was about to watch his own body being smashed into atoms and burned to ashes.

Then something swept him upwards, and he flew into the skies so fast that he thought he was going to heaven.

He wasn't!

Pursuit in the Skies

Roger Wilde, also known as Sky Captain, flung his flying suit with a hard sweeping fling of his arms hard left, just as a heat seeking missile from a Swash jet bomber smashed through the space he had been flying. His position adaptors straightened him again into a proper flying position once the danger was safely past and he tongued his helmet control to urge more speed out of his flying suit.

"Damn!" Roger cursed.

"Roger?"

"Swash jet bomber, Barry."

"Already?"

"Yeah. I guess they got out of the party early, pal."

"Sucks."

"Pretty much."

"What now?"

"Not sure yet."

Roger angled lower, losing speed rapidly.

The Swash jet bomber hurtled past, unable to slow as quickly.

"Got an idea."

Barry laughed. "Let them kill you?"

"Nah. Then you'd take up both beds in our room."

"Fat chance of that. But I'd be happy to eat your rations."

The Swash jet bomber fired two rockets this time.

Roger's helmet radar lit up. "Targeted, Barry!"

"Oh crap!" Barry shot back.

Roger palmed a button his chest.

An image of Al and Tesla showed up in his mind's eye. "Don't press the green button unless your ass is just about kicked from here to Timbuktu!"

Roger grinned. "Timbuktu!"

He let go the button.

Wham!

The two rockets passed through a vanishing image of Roger and his Sky Captain suit.

Nuclear Destruction

Sky Captain shot out of a telescoping burst of energies above an air force base, dark and silent.

He eyed it carefully.

"Barry, I seem to be over an American air force base."

Noise.

"Barry, do you copy me?"

Static and noise.

Roger sighed. What had just happened to him?

He angled lower and then slowed to a crawl then landed before what was plainly a commissary building. You could always tell; they were the only building sporting a flag and surrounded by lots of empty or full parking spaces.

He dropped to the ground.

Then he walked several paces and looked up at a sign over the building: Mather Air Force Commissary.

"Oh crap!" Roger cursed.

"Barry!" He practically screamed. This was impossible. All the major air force bases had been nuked during the first strike by Hitler's bombs.

Then he blacked out.

Roger struggled against the maglocks that kept him chained to the wall. Barry watched him from across the cell, straining against his own as well. Finally, they both stopped.

"Well if that doesn't take the cake." Barry finally said in a blast of exhaustion and frustration.

Both men had been strung up to the wall now for two days without food or water. Their pants were soiled and stinking and their arms hurt like hell as well. Their wrists and hands were going number. Their legs were about to buckle, which meant they would probably collapse, causing their wrists to dislocate and the loss of both hands.

"Yeah. War stinks." Roger cursed. "And so, do we?"

"Well, the way I see it, pal, is that if the Black Guard don't turn us into Zombies to kill our friends, then these Eastern Faction crazies going to rip our skin off to see what makes us tick."

"Or both." Roger added.

"You had to say that, didn't you? Didn't you!" Barry shot back.

"Hey! Someone's gotta keep up our spirits!"

"War is still hell."

"And it stinks!" Roger said sniffing the air in a comical manner.

"Now, now Roger. Just look at it as a little manly fragrance to pass the time away with."

"This is serious." Roger insisted.

"And it's never not been?"

"Noted."

Roger sighed, and then looked to the solid wall that opened to allow their captors inside. "What do you think they want from us?"

"Maybe a chocolate malted and fries."

Roger laughed despite himself. "Barry!"

"Yeah man. Thinking. Thinking." Shakes his head. "Nope. No thoughts. You?"

Before Roger could reply to the door in the wall slid open, revealing a very beautiful oriental woman clad in a doctor's smock. Her hands were covered in gloves.

"This don't look good, Roger." Barry said, eyeing the gloves.

"Losing your touch with the ladies, Barry?"

"In this case I'll make an exception." Barry quipped, again his eyes not leaving those gloved hands. Finally, he looked up. "I hope those gloves have got useful purposes...like letting us out of our prison, feeding us, arming us."

The oriental woman neither smiled, nor responded. She came into the room, plucked a thermometer from her smock, stuck it in Roger's mouth, then went to the other side of the room and did the same with Barry.

Barry smiled at her. "My favorite flavor. None."

Her eyes flickered for a moment, but she still said nothing. She left the room.

Roger looked over at Barry. "I think your charm is making headway."

"Yeah. Like an airplane crash."

They both laughed.

Several minutes later the door opened again, and the same oriental woman entered the room, plucked the thermometers out, made a note of their temperatures, and then exited again.

"What the hell?" Barry asked no one in particular.

"You have to admit, it does help pass the time between getting nowhere fast and possibly being tortured next."

Barry perked up. "You think?"

Roger didn't respond. He didn't want to think about it. He knew what kind of tortures the Orientals on his own timeline had used during World War Two; he could only imagine what the ones in this crazy cocked up would do.

The door opened again a large man, also in a doctor's smock entered. He was glancing at a notepad in his hands. He was escorted by what appeared to be Samurai, except that instead of swords they carried these wicked looking rods with barbed tips that emitted sparks every now and then.

Barry swallowed. The torture was about to begin.

The large man gestured to Barry.

The guards headed for him.

"Roger!"

"Don't worry, pal. I'll be there with you when the time comes."

Barry looked back at Roger as he was removed from the maglocks. "You're kidding? Right? Right?"

As the guards walked past Roger, he suddenly jerked his entire body upwards, straining against the maglocks with his hands to hold on, and kicked the nearest Samurai Guard. It swung around and shoved its rod at Roger, who managed to dodge the blow to his chest. The rod glanced across his shoulder and struck the maglocks over Roger's head, emitting a shower of sparks.

Roger slumped against the wall.

"Damn! Roger! Roger!" Barry cried out as the Samurai Guard gave Roger a second blast from his rod in his back, then grunted happily and followed the first guard and the large man out. The doors closed.

Roger's body hung on the maglocks for what seemed like forever, but then a strange thing occurred. A smile slid across his lips.

Zombie Factory

Barry was hauled into a large warehouse with an open door at the opposite end, where Japanese Soldiers were marching. Rows of odd-looking tanks lined opposite walls. The tanks cannon all appeared like the rods the guards carried. He was marched to a large table where his and Roger's jump suits lay stretched out. A scientist with a Black Guard band on his right upper arm, with its red deadhead on it, looked up from his examination of the suits.

"Ah, I see you have accepted our invitation to join us." The scientist said. He nodded to the large man, and he walked off. The two guards fell back from Barry, who began rubbing his wrists to bring life into them again. He hadn't had a chance in the grip of the guards.

"I wasn't invited." Barry said, his voice growling and low.

"Come now. Surely you can appreciate a bit of humor considering what we could alternatively choose to do?"

"You mean like hanging me on a wall and torturing me?"

"Oh no, that would be too uncivilized."

The scientist gestured to the right and then Barry saw the silent men and women in uniform that stood at perfect attention. Their faces rigid and immobile, fists clenched against their hips. They wore Black Guard armbands.

"Zombies!" Barry uttered, the horror of what he was seeing gripping his heart and soul.

"Ah. I see you have fond memories of the good old days."

"How could you know...?"

The scientist came closer to Barry and looked into his eyes. "Do you not recognize the one who made you?"

Barry's horror grew even more. "Doctor Zombie"

Doctor Zombie smiled at Barry. "Oh, I'm so much more than that!"

Barry managed to shake off both his guards for a moment as he rushed the Doctor, but their reactions were faster than his and they snapped him back against them again, locking their hand tightly about his arms.

The Doctor smiled. Their grips relaxed.

Barry tensed, ready to spring again for the Doctor, but decided to see if a better moment would arise.

"Yes. A curious name your fellow zombies named me and one I've grown affectionate of. And I have never forgotten you, Barry. You always were the one that got away. Both figuratively and literally in the end. I look forward to inspecting your brain to see how that happened." He clapped his hands.

The guards gripped Barry by his arms again. He tried to shake them off but was too weak to do so. Their strength was immense.

"I see you have noticed the superior strength of my new generation." The scientist said.

"You're mad." Barry swore. "No good will ever come from this!"

"Oh, but it already has. I expect you to talk excitedly about these..." He pointed to the jump suits. "And very loudly."

One of the guards quite unexpectedly broke Barry's left pinkie.

Barry screamed in pain.

"Am I making myself quite clear, Barry?"

"But how, how did he know to..." Barry uttered despite his growing pain.

The scientist tapped his head. "Here. I have found a way to connect myself to all my creations."

And upon those words every single zombie in the lineups turned and saluted the scientists with a Black Guard goosestep to boot.

"Damn!" Barry muttered, a smile coming to his lips. "Busby Berkeley could sure use these guys!"

Barry screamed even louder when his left pinkie was broken.

"What the hell you do that for, man?" Barry hollered.

The scientist tapped his head. "Because I can. Now, shall we talk as peace loving men, or shall we continue our little game of sticks and stones."

The scientist started to smile and then grimaced and made a very, very ugly face as his forehead sprouted a blossom of red. He tumbled to the concrete floor and lay there unmoving.

Barry broke away from the guards, expecting them to stop him, but they were frozen in place. Alarms began to ring.

Roger came running from behind a tank, tossing a Japanese rifle to the ground as he dashed Barry's way. "Suit up!" He screamed.

Barry didn't wait for another invitation. He hurriedly buttoned up as Roger scrambled to do his own. Both men finished as the troops arrived. A barrage of bullets zinged about them. They didn't wait for further encouragement.

"Rockets away!" Roger hollered.

"You got it!" Barry cried out.

Both men ran towards the exit, where the massive doors were beginning to close with a loud groaning sound. They leaped into the air and their rockets cut in and propelled them faster and faster towards the diminishing exit opening.

Soldiers outside were running to cover the exit, firing at them as they came closer.

"Ever had a close shave before, Barry."

"Yeah...every day with you!" Barry cursed.

Then both men in perfect sync turned as one sideways and shot out the closing door exit, making it just in the nick of time. The soldiers outside spun around and aimed their weapons at the fleeing men, firing round after round.

"Ow!" Barry cried out as they shot over the encampment and the vast warehouse, they had been held captive in.

"Where you shot, Barry?"

"My damn pinkies, they're both broken, and I forgot that and tried to use them."

"Next time, use your middle finger." Roger joked.

Barry did. But not on his controls.

The two rocket men shot upwards and safely into the high clouds overhead.

Don't miss out!

Visit the website below and you can sign up to receive emails whenever John Pirillo publishes a new book. There's no charge and no obligation.

https://books2read.com/r/B-A-EMSD-OZIQC

BOOKS 2 READ

Connecting independent readers to independent writers.

Did you love *Sky Captain Adventures 2, Zombie World*? Then you should read *Arch of Time*[1] by John Pirillo!

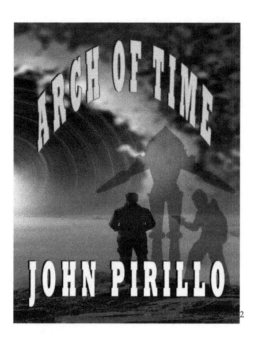

[2]

Rocket Man...a hero rises to fight against the evil empire of the Third Reich in a thrilling new series of books.

Harry is an Air Force test pilot. An ordinary guy most of the time. But his passion for flying is going to test him in more ways than planned when he becomes involved in a top-secret WorldWar Two program.

Run by the great Albert Einstein and Nikola Tesla, Harry is about to step out of his life as a loving husband and fatherinto a world that spans space and time.

He is going to become the most powerful man to have ever lived and a weapon that will makethe Axis of Evil tremble with fear!

Four books in one enormous collection that takes you from Harry's beginning during World War Twoto the distant future of World War Three.

---

1. https://books2read.com/u/brBXX7

2. https://books2read.com/u/brBXX7

A family man and a brilliant engineer, Harry, is determinied to help do anything and everything possible towin World War Two.

The last thing he could ever expected to happen was that he would become a weapon of war himself...as Rocket Man.

A powerful flying suit that would allow Harry to fly faster than a speeding rocket, and bring the war back to HItler and

is minions in a powerful way.

No one was certain the suit worked until Hitler sent one of his advanced bombers to San Francisco to test a tactical nuclear weapon...then all bets were off and Harry had to fly the suit or lose everything and everyone he loved!

FIRST STRIKE, SAN FRANCISCO

PHOENIX

PHONENIX RISING

THE LONG WAR

If you like action-packed science fiction adventures and a time travel tale that spans centuries...this book is going to make your heart pound

with excitement.

Read more at www.johnpirillo.com.

Also by John Pirillo

Angel Hamilton
Broken Fangs

Baker Street Universe Tales
Baker Street Universe Tales
Baker Street Universe Tales 2
Baker Street Universe Tales 3
Baker Street Universe Tales 4
Baker Street Universe Tales 5
Baker Street Universe Tales 6
Baker Street Universe Tales Seven

BAKER STREET WIZARD
Baker Street Wizard 4
Baker Street Wizard 5

Between
Prince of Between

"Classic Baker Street Universe Sherlock Holmes"
Sherlock Holme: Hyde's Night of Terror
Case of the Deadly Goddess
Case of the Abominable

Cythulhu
The Cthulhu Incident
The Eye of Cthulhu
The Throne of Cythulhu
Throne of Cthulhu
Giants of Cythulhu

Deadly
Sherlock Holmes, Deadly Master
Sherlock Holmes, Deadly Magic

Detective Judge Dee
Detective Dee Murder Most Chaste

Double Holmes
Sherlock Holmes, Double Holmes 2
Double Holmes 7
Double Holmes 8
Double Holmes 9
Double Holmes 10
Double Holmes 11
Double Holmes 12

Double Holmes 13
Double Holmes 14
Double Holmes 15

Elektron
Elektron

Escape To Adventure
Escape to Adventure
Escape to Atlantis

FRACTAL UNIVERSE
Twist
Portal

G1, The Bureau of Extraordinary Investigations
Shifter 2+
Shifter 3+

Gears World
Gears World 5

Halloween
Sherlock Holmes, Halloween Monsters 2
Halloween Treats

Sherlock Holmes, Halloween Vampire Tales
Sherlock Holmes, Halloween Werewolf Tales

Hollow Earth Special Forces
Hollow Earth Special Forces, Forbidden World
Operation Deep Thrust
The Ancients

Holmes
Sherlock Holmes Struck
Sherlock Holmes A Dangerous Act

Infinite Tales
Infinite Tales 3
Infinite Tales 4
Infinite Tales 5
Infinite Tales 6
Infinite Tales 7
Infinite 8
Infinite Tales 9
Infinite Tales
Infinite Tales Two

Monster Hunter
Monster Hunter

Mystery Knight

HellBound Mystery
Hell Bound Angel

PhaseShift
PhaseShift
PhaseShift Two: Crossover
PhaseShift: Shifting Worlds

Rocketman
Rocketman
Rocket Man, Time Streams
Rocketman Christmas
Time Wars
Arch of Time

Secret Adventures of Jules Verne and Alexander Dumas
Hollow Earth
Hollow Earth

Sherlock Holmes
Sherlock Holmes, ICE
The Ice Man
Sherlock Holmes Fallen
Sherlock Holmes: Monster
Sherlock Holmes: Tick Tock
Sherlock Holmes Christmas Magic
Sherlock Holmes Dark Secret
Sherlock Holmes Shadow of Dorian Gray
Sherlock Holmes Vampire

Sherlock Holmes: Cursed in Stone
Sherlock Holmes Apparition
Sherlock Holmes Case of the Raging Madness
Sherlock Holmes Dark Princess
Sherlock Holmes Dark Angel
Constable Evans' Fancy
Sherlock Holmes Matter of Perception
Sherlock Holmes Tangled
Sherlock Holmes Case of the Gossamer Lady
Sherlock Holmes House of Shadows
Sherlock Holmes The Yellow Death
Sherlock Holmes Oblique
Sherlock Holmes Mystery Train Winter Collection
Sherlock Holmes A Tale Less Told
Sherlock Holmes Mystery Six
Sherlock Holmes, Rules of Darkness, Special Edition
Sherlock Holmes Shape of Justice
Sherlock Holmes Christmas Magic
Sherlock Holmes Fallen Angel
Ghostly Shadows
Sherlock Holmes Bloody Hell
Sherlock Holmes Monster of the Tower
Sherlock Holmes Darkest of Nights
Sherlock Holmes Nightmare
Sherlock Holmes Poetry of Death
Sherlock Holmes, Dracula
Sherlock Holmes #3, Ice Storm
Sherlock Holmes, Baker Street Wizard 3

Sherlock Holmes Double Holmes
Sherlock Holmes, Double Holmes 1

Sherlock Holmes, Mammoth Fantasy, Murder and Mystery Tales
Sherlock Holmes, Mammoth Fantasy, Murder, and Mystery Tales 15
Sherlock Holmes Mammoth Fantasy, Murder, and Mystery Tales 17
Sherlock Holmes Mammoth Fantasy, Murder, and Mystery Tales 26
Sherlock Holmes Mammoth Fantasy, Murder, and Mystery Tales 14

Sherlock Holmes, Mammoth Fantasy, Murder, and Mystery Tales 15
Sherlock, Holmes, Mammoth Fantasy, Murder, and Mystery Tales 15

Sherlock Holmes Urban Fantasy Mysteries
Sherlock Holmes Urban Fantasy Mysteries
Sherlock Holmes, Halloween Monsters
Sherlock Holmes Urban Fantasy Mysteries 2
Sherlock Holmes Urban Fantasy Mysteries 3
Sherlock Holmes, Urban Fantasy Mysteries 3
Sherlock Holmes Urban Fantasy Mysteries 4
Sherlock Holmes, Artifact
Sherlock Holmes, The Dracula Files
Sherlock Holmes, Dark Clues
Sherlock Holmes, Case of the Undying Man
Sherlock Holmes, Mystery of the Sea
Sherlock Holmes, Night Watch
Sherlock Holmes, Mystery of the Path not Taken
Sherlock Holmes, the Dorian Gray Affair
The Baker Street Universe
Sherlock Holmes, The Dracula Affair
Spector
Sherlock Holmes, Rules of Darkness
Sherlock Holmes, A Tale Less Told
Sherlock Holmes, The Christmas Star

Sherlock Holmes, Christmas Tales
Steampunk Holmes
Sherlock HOlmes, Deadly Valentine's Day
Sherlock Holmes, Angel Murders
Sherlock Holmes, Deadly Intent
Sherlock Holmes, White Diamond Mystery
Sherlock Holmes, Gears World, Box Set One
Sherlock Holmes, The Blue Fire of Harry Houdini
Sherlock Holmes, White Diamond Vampire Mystery
Sherlock Holmes, Black Tower
Sherlock Holmes, Tales of the Macabre
Sherlock Holmes, Baker Street Wizard
Sherlock Holmes, Usher
Sherlock Holmes, Baker Street Wizard 2
Sherlock Holmes, Double Holmes 1
Sherlock Holmes, Cave of the Dark Elf
Sherlock Holmes, Something Wicked
Sherlock Holmes, Gears Word 3
Sherlock Holmes, Gears World 4
Sherlock Holmes, Deadly
Sherlock Holmes, Urban Fantasy Mysteries Six
Werewolves
Sherlock Holmes, Mammoth Fantasy, Murder, and Mystery Tales 27
Sherlock Holmes, Urban Fantasy Mysteries
Sherlock Holmes, Lord of the Trees

Sherlock Holmes, Urban Fantasy Mystery Tales
Sherlock Holmes, Urban Fantasy Mystery Tales 2
Sherlock Holmes, Dark Matters

Sky Captain Adventures
Sky Captain Adventures 2, Zombie World

Steampunk Holmes
Sherlock Holmes, Gears of the Goddess

The Baker Street Detective
The Baker Street Detective 5, The Howling Wind
Strange Times, The Baker Street Detective, Book2
The Baker Street Detective, Hollow Man
Sherlock Holmes, Baker Street Detectives

Thrilling Mystery Tales
Thrilling Mystery Tales 2

Twist
Twist 2
Twister

Urban Fantasies
Urban Fantasies 1
Urban Fantasies 3
Urban Fantasies

War of the Worlds
Battle for Earth

WireShip
Wirestation Red Lion

Standalone
Sherlock Holmes Deadly Consequences
Invisibility Factor
Red Painted Souls
Between
Robin Hood
Shadow Man
The Rainbow Bridge
Cartoon, Johnnie Angel
Sherlock Holmes 221B
Sherlock Holmes Shape Shifter
Urban Fantasy Mysteries
Sherlock Holmes, Urban Fantasy Mysteries
Halloween Mysteries
Invasion
Romancing the Word
Romancing the Word Workbook
Sherlock Holmes, Gears World 2
Thrilling Mystery Tales
Weird Short Tales
Spectre Forces
Young King Arthur
Dark Midnight
Anomalies
Shifter+
Shifter 4+
Deep Silence
Sherlock Holmes, Halloween Fantasies
Sherlock Holmes, Halloween Terror

Sherlock Holmes, Halloween Terror 2

Watch for more at www.johnpirillo.com.